next door

(a chloe fine psychological suspense—book 1)

blake pierce

Copyright © 2018 by Blake Pierce. All rights reserved. Except as permitted under the U.S. Copyright Act of 1976, no part of this publication may be reproduced, distributed or transmitted in any form or by any means, or stored in a database or retrieval system, without the prior permission of the author. This ebook is licensed for your personal enjoyment only. This ebook may not be re-sold or given away to other people. If you would like to share this book with another person, please purchase an additional copy for each recipient. If you're reading this book and did not purchase it, or it was not purchased for your use only, then please return it and purchase your own copy. Thank you for respecting the hard work of this author. This is a work of fiction. Names, characters, businesses, organizations, places, events, and incidents either are the product of the author's imagination or are used fictionally. Any resemblance to actual persons, living or dead, is entirely coincidental. Jacket image Copyright Jan Faukner, used under license from Shutterstock.com.
ISBN: 978-1-64029-598-8

BOOKS BY BLAKE PIERCE

BEFORE HE HUNTS (Book #8)
BEFORE HE PREYS (Book #9)
BEFORE HE LONGS (Book #10)

AVERY BLACK MYSTERY SERIES
CAUSE TO KILL (Book #1)
CAUSE TO RUN (Book #2)
CAUSE TO HIDE (Book #3)
CAUSE TO FEAR (Book #4)
CAUSE TO SAVE (Book #5)
CAUSE TO DREAD (Book #6)

KERI LOCKE MYSTERY SERIES
A TRACE OF DEATH (Book #1)
A TRACE OF MUDER (Book #2)
A TRACE OF VICE (Book #3)
A TRACE OF CRIME (Book #4)
A TRACE OF HOPE (Book #5)

PROLOGUE

Chloe sat on the front steps of her apartment building beside her twin sister, Danielle, watching as the police led their father down the front stoop, in handcuffs.

A large cop with a round belly stood in front of Chloe and Danielle. His black skin glistened with sweat as the summer night beamed down on them.

"You girls don't need to see this," he said.

Chloe thought it was a silly thing to say. Even at ten years old, she knew he was simply trying to block out the sight of their father being led into the back of a cop car.

That sight was the least of her problems. She'd already seen the blood at the bottom of the stairs. She'd seen how it was splattered on the bottom step and then soaked into the carpet that led into the living room. She'd seen the body, too. It had been facedown. Her father had tried very hard not to let her see it. But no matter what he did, the sight of all that blood had stuck itself to the walls of her head.

It was what she saw as the fat cop stood in front of her. It was all that she saw.

Chloe heard the door to the police car slam closed. She knew it was the sound of her father leaving them—she sensed, forever.

"You girls okay?" the cop asked.

Neither of them answered. Chloe was still seeing all of that blood at the bottom of the stairs, soaking into the blue carpet. She looked quickly over at Danielle and saw that her sister was staring at her feet. She wasn't blinking. Chloe was pretty sure something was wrong with her. Chloe thought Danielle had seen more of the body, maybe even the really dark spot where all of the blood seemed to have come from.

The fat cop looked up the front stoop stairs all of a sudden. Under his breath, he said in a hissing voice: "Christ, can't you wait? The girls are right here…"

Behind the cop, they brought a body bag out of the building and down the steps. It was the body. The one that had leaked all of that dark red blood on the carpet.

Their mother.

1

"Girls?" the cop asked. "One of you want to talk to me?"

But Chloe did not want to talk.

Sometime later, a familiar car pulled up behind one of the remaining cop cars. The fat cop had stopped trying to get them to talk and Chloe sensed that he was just there with them so they would not feel alone.

Beside Chloe, Danielle said her first word since they had been brought out to the front stoop.

"Grandma," Danielle said.

The familiar car that had showed up belonged to their grandmother. She got out of the car as quickly as her legs would allow. Chloe saw that she was crying.

She felt a tear sliding down her face but it was not like crying. It felt like something breaking.

"Your grandmother is here," the cop said. He sounded relieved, happy to be rid of them.

"Girls," was the only word her grandmother got out as she came up the stairs. After that, she started to sob and took both of her granddaughters in an awkward embrace.

Oddly enough, it was that embrace that Chloe would remember.

The sight of the blood would become faint. The fat cop faded after just a few weeks, as did the surreal sight of the cuffs.

But for her entire life, Chloe would remember that awkward hug.

And the feeling of something deep inside cracking, and then breaking.

Had her father truly killed her mother?

CHAPTER ONE

17 Years Later

Chloe Fine climbed up the stairs of her new home—the home that she and her fiancé had hunted for, for months—and she could hardly contain her excitement.

"That box too heavy?"

Steven dashed up the steps beside her, carrying a box labeled PILLOWS.

"Not at all," she said, hefting her own box, which read DISHES on the side.

Steven set his box down and took hers.

"Let's trade," he said with a smile.

He had been smiling a lot recently. Actually, there seemed to have been a permanent smile on his face ever since she had allowed him to slip an engagement ring on her finger eight months ago.

They marched together up the sidewalk. As they went, Chloe took in the sight of the yard. It wasn't the big sprawling yard she'd always envisioned. In her mind, her house had a big open yard with trees scattered along the back. Instead, she and Steven had settled on one in a quiet neighborhood. But she was only twenty-seven; she had time. Both she and Steven knew that this was not the house they'd grow old in. And something about that made it even more special. This was to be their starter home, the place they would learn the ins and outs of marriage—and maybe where they'd work at having a kid or two.

She could see their neighbor's house quite clearly. The lawns were separated only by a series of tall bushes. The picturesque white porch was almost identical to their own.

"I know I grew up here for the most part," Chloe said. "But it just doesn't feel the same. It feels like a different town."

"I assure you, it's exactly the same," Steven said. "Well, give or take a few new housing developments like the one we are currently homeowners in. Good old Pinecrest, Maryland. Small enough so you'll always run into people you don't want to but just large enough to not have to drive an hour to a grocery store."

"I miss Philly already."

"Not me," Steven said. "No more Eagles fans, no more Rocky jokes, no more traffic."

"All good points," Chloe agreed. "Still…"

"Give it some time," Steven said. "This will feel like home soon enough."

Chloe wished her grandmother was there in that moment to see this house. Chloe was pretty sure she'd be proud. She'd probably also waste no time in firing up the brand new oven in the kitchen in order to bake a celebratory dessert.

But she'd died two years ago, just ten months after Chloe's grandfather died in a car accident. It would have been poetic to think she'd died of a broken heart but that hadn't been the case; in the end, it was a heart attack that claimed her grandmother.

Chloe also thought of Danielle. Right after high school, Danielle had moved away to Boston for a few years. There had been a pregnancy scare, an arrest or two, and several failed jobs. All of that had eventually led her sister back here, to Pinecrest, a few years ago.

As for Chloe, she had gone to college in Philadelphia, met Steven, and started working toward her career of becoming an FBI agent. She had a few classes remaining, but the transition had been smooth. Baltimore was just a half hour drive to the west and all of her credits had transferred without a hitch.

The stars had seemed to align in some majestic way when Steven had managed to land a job in Pinecrest. As much as Chloe joked about not wanting to return to Pinecrest, something inside of her knew she'd always end up back there if even for just a few years. It was a dumb sentiment but she felt she owed it to her grandparents. Growing up, she couldn't get out of this place fast enough and she felt that her grandparents had always taken that a little personally.

And then the perfect house had come along and Chloe had started to love the idea of being back in a smaller town. Pinecrest wasn't tiny at all—a population of about thirty-five thousand made it a comfortable size as far as Chloe was concerned.

Also, she was excited to meet up with Danielle at some point.

But first, they had to finish moving in. The meager belongings she and Steven owned were packed into the back of the U-Haul that was currently parked askew in their small concrete driveway. They were now two hours into unloading the truck, in and out, back and forth, until they could finally see the back of the trailer through the last row of boxes and bins.

As Steven brought in the last of the boxes, Chloe began to unpack. It was surreal to realize that these were items from their separate apartments now being unboxed to share the same space they'd share as a couple. It was a warm feeling, one that made her glance at the ring on her finger with a confident smile.

As she was unpacking, she heard a knock on the front door—the first actual knock at their new home. This was followed by a woman's high-pitched voice saying: *"Hello?"*

Confused, Chloe stopped unpacking and walked to the front door. She wasn't sure what she was expecting to see but it certainly wasn't a face from her past. Strangely enough, that's exactly what she found waiting at the door.

"Chloe Fine?" the woman asked.

It had been eight years, but Chloe recognized the face of Kathleen Saunders easily enough. They'd gone to high school together. It was very dreamlike to see her here, standing at her front door. While not the best of friends in high school, they had been a bit more than casual acquaintances. Still, seeing a face from her past standing in the threshold of her future was so unexpected that it made Chloe feel dizzy for a moment.

"Kathleen?" she asked. "What the hell are you doing here?"

"Living here," Kathleen said with a smile. She had put on quite a bit of weight since high school but her smile was exactly the same.

"Here?" Chloe asked. "In this neighborhood?"

"Yes. Two houses over, to your right. I was coming in from walking my dog and I *thought* it was you. Well, you or your sister. So I came over and asked the man in the back of the U-Haul and he said to come on up and say hello. Is that your husband?"

"Fiancé," Chloe said.

"Well, how small of a world is this?" she asked. "Or…rather, how small of a *town*."

"Yes, I suppose it really is," Chloe said.

"I'd love to stay and chat, but I actually have to go meet with a client in about an hour," Kathleen said. "And besides, I don't want to keep you from unpacking. But listen…there's a block party this Saturday. I wanted to be the first to personally invite you."

"Well, thanks. I appreciate it."

"Hey, really quickly…how's Danielle? I know when she finished up high school she was going through some stuff. Rumor has it that she's living in Boston."

"She *was* in Boston," Chloe said. "But she's actually been back here in Pinecrest for a few years."

"That's so cool," Kathleen said. "Maybe invite her to the block party, too? I'd love to get to catch up with both of you!"

"Likewise," Chloe said.

She briefly looked over Kathleen's shoulder and saw Steven in the back of the U-Haul. He was shrugging his shoulders and giving a squinted up face that seemed to say: *I'm sorry!*

"Well, it was so good to see you," Kathleen said. "I hope to see you at the block party. And if not, you know where I live!"

"Yup! Two houses over, to the right."

Kathleen nodded and then surprised Chloe with a hug. Chloe returned it, pretty sure Kathleen had not been the hugging type back in high school. She watched her old (and new, she supposed) friend wave to Steven as she walked back down to the sidewalk along the street.

Steven came back up the porch steps, carrying the final two boxes. Chloe took the top one off for him and they carried them into the living room. The place was a maze of boxes, bins, and luggage.

"Sorry about that," Steven said. "I didn't know if that would be a welcome guest or not."

"No, it's fine. It was *weird,* but fine."

"She said she was a friend from high school?"

"Yeah. And here we are, living two houses apart. She seemed really sweet, though. She invited us to a block party this weekend."

"That's nice."

"She knew Danielle back in high school, too. I think I'm going to invite her to the party, too."

Steven started opening up one of the boxes, letting out a sigh. "Chloe, we haven't even been here an entire day. Can't we wait before inviting your sister into our lives?"

"We are," she said. "The party is three days away. So we're waiting three days."

"You know what I mean. Danielle has a tendency to make things difficult when they don't have to be."

Chloe *did* know what he meant. Steven had met Danielle four times and each of those occasions had been awkward—and neither of them had a problem saying as much. Danielle came with a particular set of issues, none of which were well suited for being

6

around people she was unfamiliar with. So she supposed Steven was right. Why invite her to a block party where she wouldn't know anyone?

But the answer was easy: *Because she's my sister. She's been alone and hurting these last few years and as lame as it sounds, she needs me.*

A quick flash of the two of them sitting on those apartment stairs tore through her head like a desert wind.

"You knew I'd reach out to her eventually," Chloe said. "I can't very well be living in the same city and continue to shut her out of my life."

Steven nodded and came to her. "I know, I know," he said. "But a man can dream."

She knew there was a bit of barbed truth to the comment but she also recognized the joking tone. He was giving in, not wanting to let a discussion about her sister ruin moving day for them.

"It could be good for her," Chloe said. "Getting out and socializing...I think I can bring it out of her if I can become something of a regular fixture in her life."

Steven knew the complex history between the two of them. And although he made no secrets about not being particularly fond of Danielle, he had always lovingly supported Chloe and understood her concern for her sister.

"Do what you think is best for her, then," he said. "And after you call her, come help me put the bed together in the master bedroom. I've got plans for it later."

"Oh, you do?"

"Yeah. All this moving has wiped me out. I'm exhausted, I'm going to sleep so hard...and it's going to be so hot."

They both cracked up and found their way into each other's arms. They shared a lingering kiss that suggested maybe their first night in their new home *would* put the bed to good use. But for now, there were the mounds and mounds of boxes to unpack.

Plus, a potentially uncomfortable phone call to make to her sister.

It was a thought that filled her with equal amounts of joy and anxiousness.

Even as her twin sister, Chloe was never sure what to expect from Danielle. And something about being back in Pinecrest made her sadly certain that things with Danielle had likely only gotten worse.

CHAPTER TWO

Danielle Fine popped a No-Doz, swallowed it down with a warm, flat Coke, then opened up her underwear drawer and dug down on the right side for the sluttiest thing she could find.

Danielle thought about Martin. They had been dating for about six weeks now. And while they had both decided that they were going to take it slow, Danielle had lost her patience. She had decided she was going to throw herself at him tonight; stopping at second base every time they saw one another was making her feel like a stupid teenager who didn't know what she was doing.

She knew what she was doing. And she was pretty sure Martin did, too. By the end of the night, she'd know for sure.

She ended up selecting a lacy black pair that barely covered the front and was practically nonexistent in the back. She thought about which bra to wear but decided on not wearing one at all. She and Martin weren't exactly dress-up types and besides, she knew she was very much lacking in the chest; there was no expensive bra in the world that was going to be of much help. Besides…Martin had told her he liked how her boobs looked when their shapes were visible through a T-shirt.

They were meeting early, catching an early dinner so they could make the 6:30 movie in time. The mere fact that they were doing dinner and a movie rather than cheap drinks and a trip back to his house for a painful make-out session was a point in her favor. She wondered if Martin was the kind who liked to feel that he was being a gentleman.

Six weeks with the guy…you should already know that kind of shit, she thought as she slid on the panties.

She got dressed in front of the full-length mirror on her bedroom wall. She tried on a few shirts before deciding to play it chill. She settled for a black, slightly tight T-shirt and a very basic pair of jeans. She was not the sort of girl who owned a bunch of dresses or skirts. She normally put on the first thing she grabbed in the morning. She knew she'd been blessed with her mother's good looks and, because she also managed to have immaculate skin, she usually went without much makeup, too. Her dyed black hair and intense brown eyes pulled the entire package together; in the blink of an eye she could make the transformation from innocent and sweet to aggressively sexy. It was one of the reasons she had never really cared about her small boobs.

With a quick look into the mirror, seeing the same figure, face, and T-shirt band logo that had all been there as a teen, Danielle was ready to head out to meet Martin. He was a greaseball of sorts, only not the kind that hung out in motor garages or racetracks. He'd toyed with amateur boxing at one point, or so he said. He had the body to make her believe it (another reason she was losing her patience) and currently worked as a freelance IT specialist. But, like her, he didn't take life too seriously and enjoyed drinking a lot. So far, they seemed like a perfect match.

But still. Six weeks without sex. She felt a lot of pressure. What if he refused? What if he really wanted to keep taking it slow and she just couldn't wait?

Sighing, she went to the fridge. To calm her nerves, she grabbed a Guinness from the fridge, popped the top, and took a swig. She realized she was putting alcohol on top of her No-Doz but shrugged it off. She'd certainly put her body through much worse.

Her phone rang. *If he's calling to cancel on me, I'll kill him,* she thought.

When she saw that it wasn't his name on the display, she relaxed. Yet when she saw it was her sister, she slumped her shoulders. She knew she might as well answer it. If she didn't Chloe would call her back fifteen minutes from now. Persistence was one of the few traits they had in common.

She answered the call, skipping hellos as she usually did. "Welcome back to Pinecrest," she said, as monotone as possible. "You officially a resident again?"

"Depends on if you're asking me or all of these unpacked boxes," Chloe replied.

"When did you get in?" Danielle asked.

"This morning. We finally got everything out of the U-Haul and are trying to get through the boxes and figure out where everything needs to go."

"Do you need some help?" Danielle asked.

The brief silence on the other end of the line suggested that Chloe had not been expecting this sort of generosity. Truth be told, Danielle had only asked because she knew Chloe would not take her up on it. Or, rather, Steven would not *want* Chloe to take her up on it.

9

"You know, I think we're good right now. I wish I would have thought to call you when we were unpacking all of the damned boxes."

"Maybe I wouldn't have offered then," Danielle said with dry sarcasm.

"Anyway, listen. Do you remember Kathleen Saunders from high school?"

"Vaguely," Danielle said, the name bringing to mind a bright and smiling teenaged face—the kind of face that always got a little too close when speaking.

"Turns out she lives in my neighborhood. Just two houses down. She came by a while ago and said hello. She also invited Steven and I to a block party this weekend."

"Wow, one day in and you already sound domesticated as hell. You buy a minivan yet?"

There was another brief silence; Danielle figured Chloe was trying to decide if the comment was a venomous barb or just a joke. "Not yet," she finally answered. "Need the babies first. But about that block party…I think you should come. Kathleen was asking about you."

"I'm flattered," Danielle said, not flattered at all.

"Look, we're going to end up hanging out anyway," Chloe said. "We may as well do it sooner rather than later to avoid all the phone tag. And I'd really like for you to see the house."

"I might have a date that day," Danielle said.

"Like a real date or just one of your poor one-night guys?"

"A real date. You'd like him, I think." That was bullshit. She was pretty sure Chloe wouldn't approve of Martin at all.

"You know how we can find out? Bring him, too."

"Ah Jesus, you're insufferable."

"Is that a yes?" Chloe asked.

"That's a *we'll see.*"

"I'll take it. How are you, Danielle? Everything going good?"

"Yeah, I suppose. Work is going well, and I'm about to go out on a date with the same guy for the twentieth time."

"Ooh, he *does* sound special," Chloe joked.

"Speaking of which, I need to get going," Danielle said.

"Sure. I'm going to text you our address. I hope you come to the block party. Three o'clock, this Saturday."

"No promises," Danielle said and then took a very long gulp from her Guinness. "Bye, Chloe."

She hung up without waiting for Chloe's goodbye. She had no idea why, but the conversation had been draining.

A block party, she thought with bitter sarcasm. *I know we don't talk all that often, but you'd think she'd know me better than that…*

As this thought crept through her mind, she started to think about her mother. That's where her mind usually went whenever she was irritated with Chloe. As she thought of her mom, her hand went to her neck. Finding the area there bare, she hurried back through her small apartment and into the bedroom. She went to the jewelry box on her dresser and pulled out her mother's silver necklace—just about the only tangible thing she owned that had once belonged to Gale Fine. She placed it around her neck and tucked the simple little pendant beneath her shirt.

Feeling it against her skin, she wondered how often Chloe thought of their mother. She also tried to remember the last time they had both talked about what had happened that morning seventeen years ago. She knew they were both haunted by it, but really, did anyone ever enjoy talking about ghosts?

Now with only ten minutes left before she needed to leave to meet with Martin, she chugged down the rest of her beer. She figured she could just go and be a little early. She headed for the front door to do just that but then stopped in her tracks.

Directly beneath the front door, there was an envelope. It had not been there when she was speaking on the phone with Chloe.

She walked to it and carefully picked it up. It felt like watching herself in a movie because she had done this before. This was not the first note that had come.

The envelope was unmarked. No name, no address, no markings of any kind. She opened the flap, which had not been adhered to the rest of the envelope. She reached inside and found a simple square of cardstock paper, a little larger than a playing card.

She took the note out and read it. And then read it again.

She tucked it back into the envelope and carried the envelope to the desk along the far wall of the living room. She placed it there with the other four notes, all with similar messages.

She stared at them for a moment, fearful and confused.

Her palms grew sweaty and her heart started to beat harder.

Who's watching me? she wondered. *And why?*

She then did what she usually chose to do when something bothered her. She ignored it. She pushed this most recent note out of her mind, along with the simple message it carried, and headed out the door to meet Martin.

As she walked out of the building, the note's message flashed in her mind in little shocks, almost like a neon sign.

I KNOW WHAT REALLY HAPPENED.

It made no sense, but then again, it seemed to make all the sense in the world.

She looked down at her own shadow on the city sidewalk and couldn't help but walk a little faster. She knew she could not escape a problem by putting it in her personal rearview mirror, but it at least made her feel better.

I KNOW WHAT REALLY HAPPENED.

Her feet seemed to agree, wanting to stop walking, to run back and try to make sense of the letters—to call someone. Maybe the cops. Maybe even Chloe.

But Danielle only walked faster.

She'd managed to put her past behind her, for the most part.

Why would these letters be any different?

CHAPTER THREE

"So you're still sticking with the chicken, huh?"

It was such an innocent question at its core, but it sent a flare of anger through Chloe. She lightly bit at the inside of her lip to keep any stray remarks from slipping out.

Sally Brennan, Steven's mother, was sitting across from her with an aged Stepford Wives sort of smile on her face.

"Yeah, Mom," Steven said. "It's food…food I probably won't even eat because of all the nerves. If someone wants to complain about the food at my wedding reception, then they can go home. Maybe grab some Taco Bell on the way."

Chloe squeezed Steven's hand under the table. He'd apparently picked up on her irritation. It was rare that Steven ever stood up to his mother, but when he did he came out looking like a hero.

"Well, that's not a very nice attitude to have," Sally said.

"He's right," Wayne Brennan, Steven's father, said from the other end of the table. The wine glass beside him was empty for the third time of tonight's dinner and he was reaching for the bottle of red sitting near the center of the table. "Honestly, no one gives a damn about the food at the reception. It's the booze they're looking forward to. And we'll have an open bar, so…"

They left the conversation hanging, the sour look on Sally's face making it clear that she still thought chicken was a bad choice.

But that was nothing new. She'd bitched and complained about nearly every decision Chloe and Steven had made. And she never failed to offhandedly remind them who was paying for the wedding.

As it turned out, Pinecrest was not only once again home to Chloe, but it was home to Steven's parents as well. They had moved there five years ago, technically just outside of Pinecrest in a smaller town called Elon. In addition to Steven's job, it had been one of the reasons Chloe and Steven had decided to move to Pinecrest. He worked as a software developer for a government contractor and had been offered a position that had been too good to turn down. As for Chloe, she was currently interning with the FBI while working on her master's in Criminal Justice. Because of the close proximity to FBI headquarters in Baltimore, it had all just made perfect sense

Chloe was already regretting living so close to Steven's parents, though. Wayne was all right most of the time. But Sally Brennan was, to put it mildly, an uppity bitch who loved to stick her nose in places it had no business being.

The Brennans as a couple were nice enough people, both retired, well-to-do and mostly happy. But they also coddled Steven. As an only child, Steven had admitted to Chloe numerous times that his parents had spoiled the hell out of him. Even now, when he was twenty-eight, they treated him far too much like a child. And part of that came across in an attitude of overprotectiveness. It was the main reason Chloe internally cringed whenever they wanted to go over the wedding plans.

Which, unfortunately, they apparently wanted to do over dinner. Sally had wasted no time in getting to the dinner choice for the reception.

"So how's the house?" Wayne asked, just as eager as Chloe to move away from the topic of the wedding.

"It's great," Chloe said. "We'll make it through the maze of boxes in a few days."

"Oh, and get this," Steven said. "A woman that Chloe went to high school with lives right down the street—like two houses down. Isn't that crazy?"

"Maybe not as crazy as it seems," Wayne said. "This city is just too damned small. You're bound to stumble over *someone* you know at some point."

"Especially in those neighborhoods where the houses are all on top of each other," Sally said with a smirk, making a not-so-subtle jab about their choice of location.

"Our houses aren't right on top of each other," Steven said.

"Yeah, we have a decent-sized yard," Chloe added.

Sally shrugged her shoulders and took another mouthful of wine. She then seemed to think about her next comment, maybe even almost deciding to keep it in, but letting it out anyway.

"Your high school friend isn't the only one in Pinecrest, right?" she asked. "Your sister lives around here too, if I remember correctly."

"Yes, she does."

She spoke the answer firmly but without being rude. Sally Brennan had never made any secrets about her distaste for Danielle—even though they had only ever crossed paths twice. Sally had the misfortune of being one of those clichéd bored housewives who lived for scandal and gossip. So when she found

14

that Chloe had a sister with a rocky and dark past, she'd been both appalled and intrigued.

"Let's not dwell there, Mom," Steven said.

Chloe wished this made her feel defended but if anything, it made her feel slighted. Usually when the topic of Danielle came up, Steven ended up siding with his mother. He did have the good sense to know when to shut up but his mother usually did not.

"Will she be the maid of honor?" Sally asked.

"Yes."

Sally didn't roll her eyes at the comment, but her facial expression showed her feelings about it.

"She *is* my sister," Chloe said. "So yes, I have asked her to be my maid of honor."

"Yes, it makes sense," Sally said, "but I always thought the maid of honor should be chosen carefully. It's a big honor and responsibility."

Chloe had to grip the edge of the table to keep from coming back with a hard-edged reply. Noticing her tension, Steven did his best to salvage the situation. "Mom, give it a rest," he said. "Danielle will do fine. And even if something should go wrong, I'll make sure everything is covered. This is my wedding, Mom. I'm not going to let anything bad happen."

This time it was Chloe who nearly rolled her eyes. It was once again his way of standing up for her but of also not irritating his parents. Just once, Chloe would like for him to *truly* defend Danielle. She knew that Steven had no real problems with her but that he was doing his best to pacify his mother's uneasiness of her. It was a little disgusting.

"Enough of this nonsense," Wayne said, reaching out for a second helping of the roasted potatoes. "Let's talk football. Now, Chloe…you're a Redskins fan, right?"

"God, no. Giants."

"Just as bad," Wayne said with a laugh.

And just like that, the uneasiness of the night was swept under the rug. Chloe had always valued Wayne's boldness in being able to ignore his wife's bitchiness, pushing along to some another benign topic whether she was done or not. It was a trait Chloe wished Steven had picked up from his father.

Still, as the night went on, Chloe couldn't help but wonder if Sally's worries were legitimate. Danielle was not the sort to dress up, stay quiet, and get in front of people. Danielle would be stepping out of her comfort zone at the wedding and Chloe herself had wondered how it might go over.

As those worries floated through her head, she thought of the little girls from so many years ago, sitting on the front stoop as the body bag was carried out of their apartment. She could easily recall the blank look in Danielle's face. She knew something had snapped in her at that moment. That, overnight, she had lost her sister.

And she suspected that, from that moment on, Danielle would never be the same again.

CHAPTER FOUR

It was raining when Chloe and her field work instructor arrived on the scene. She felt very minor league as she stepped out of the car into the drizzling rain. Because she was an intern having to go alongside her instructor in shifts with other interns, they were not given high-profile cases. This one, for instance, sounded as if it were a typical domestic abuse case. And while the details of the case did not sound very graphic or brutal, the very words *domestic abuse* made her cringe.

She had, after all, heard those words a lot after her mother had died. Her instructor must have been aware of her past—of what had happened with her parents—but had mentioned nothing of it this morning as they had headed out.

They were in the town of Willow Creek on that first day, a small town about fifteen miles outside of Baltimore. Chloe was interning with the FBI to eventually become part of the FBI's Evidence Response Team, and as they walked toward the simple two-story house, the instructor even let her take the lead. Her instructor was Kyle Greene, a forty-five-year-old agent who had been taken out of basic field work when he had torn his ACL while chasing down a suspect. He'd never healed properly from the injury and had been given the option to serve as an instructor and mentor of sorts for interns. He and Chloe had only spoken twice before this morning, having met via FaceTime a week ago to get to know one another and then two days ago, during her ride from Philly to Pinecrest.

"One thing before we go inside," Greene said. "I held this from you until now because I didn't want you dwelling on it all morning."

"Okay…"

"While this *is* a domestic abuse case, it is also a homicide case. When we get inside, there's going to be a body. A relatively fresh one."

"Oh…" she said, unable to contain her shock.

"I know it's more than you were expecting. But there was some discussion when you came in. Discussions to maybe let you peek behind the curtain right from the start. We've been toying with the idea of letting the interns have more responsibilities, letting them stretch out a bit more. And based on your dossier, we thought you'd be a prime candidate to test that out. I hope that's okay with you."

She was still taken aback, unable to form any real response. Yes, it was more responsibility. Yes, it meant more eyes would be on her. But she had never backed down from a challenge and she didn't intend to start now.

"I appreciate the opportunity."

"Good," Greene said, his tone indicating that he never had a doubt.

He waved her on to follow him as they walked to the porch and up the stairs. Inside, were two agents conversing with the coroner. Chloe did her best to ready herself for the scene and while she thought she'd done a pretty good job, she was still shaken when she saw a woman's legs sticking out from behind the kitchen island.

"So I need you to take a walk around the body," Greene said. "Tell me what you see—both in terms of the body and the surroundings. Walk me through your processing."

Chloe had seen a few dead bodies in the course of her interning; When she lived in Philadelphia, they had not been all that hard to come by. But this was different. This one felt a little too close to home—a little too familiar. She stepped behind the kitchen counter and looked down at the scene.

The victim was a woman who looked to be in her thirties. She had been hit in the head with a very solid object—most likely the toaster that lay shattered in pieces several feet from her. The brunt of the impact had been along the left side of her brow, hard enough to shatter the ocular cavity, making her eye look like it could very well slide out onto the floor at any moment. A pool of blood surrounded her head like a halo.

Perhaps the oddest thing about her was that her sweatpants were pulled down to her ankles and her underwear pulled down to her knees. Chloe hunkered down closer to the body and looked for any other details. She saw what looked like two small scratch marks on the side of her neck. They looked to be fresh and in the shape of fingernails.

"Where's the husband?" she asked.

"In custody," Greene said. "He's admitted to it and already told the police what happened."

"But if it's a domestic dispute, why call the FBI in?" she asked.

"Because this guy was arrested three years ago for beating up his first wife so bad that she went to the ER. But she didn't press charges. And his home computer was flagged two weeks ago for potential snuff videos."

Chloe took all of that information and applied it to what she was seeing. She interlocked it all like a puzzle and spoke her theories out loud as they came to her.

"Given this man's history, he was prone to violence. Extreme violence, if the crushed toaster is any indication. The sweatpants pushed down and underwear not quite all the way down indicates that he was trying to have sex with her here in the kitchen. Maybe they *were* having sex and she wanted it to stop. Scratch marks on her neck indicate that the sex was rough and either consensual at first or entirely unwanted."

She paused here and studied the blood. "The blood looks to be relatively fresh. I'd estimate the murder to have occurred within the last six hours."

"And what would your next steps be?" Greene asked. "If we *didn't* have this guy in custody right now and there was an active search for him, how would you follow up?"

"I'd check for evidence of intercourse. We could get his DNA and get a match. While waiting for those results, though, I'd look for things like wallets upstairs in the bedroom, hoping for a driver's license. Of course, that's if it wasn't already suspected that it was the husband. If that were the case, we could get the name from the address."

Greene smiled at her, nodding. "That's right. You'd be surprised how many rookies miss the fact that it's sort of a trick question. You're in the guy's house, so you'd already know his name. But if it *wasn't* suspected that it was the husband, you're exactly right. Also…Fine, are you okay?"

The question took her by surprise—mainly because she *wasn't* okay. She had zoned out, staring at the blood on the kitchen tile. It pulled her all the way back into her past, staring at a pool of blood drying into the carpet at the bottom of the stairs.

Without warning, she started to grow faint. She braced herself against the kitchen island, afraid she was going to puke. It was alarming and embarrassing.

Is this what I can look forward to at any remotely gruesome crime scene? At any scenes that remotely resemble what happened to Mom?

She could hear Sally in the back of her head, one of the first things she'd ever said to Chloe: *I don't know how a woman would*

19

make an exceptional agent. Especially one with your traumatic background. I wonder if that sort of stress comes home with you…

"Sorry, excuse me," she mumbled. She pushed herself off the island and ran back to the front door. She nearly fell down the porch stairs on her way to the lawn, sure she was going to throw up.

Thankfully, the fates spared her that particular embarrassment. She took a series of deep breaths, concentrating so intently on them that she almost didn't notice when Greene came quietly down the porch steps.

"There are certain cases that get to me, too," he told her. He kept a respectable distance, letting her have her space. "There are going to be scenes that are much worse. Sadly, after a while, you sort of become desensitized to it."

She nodded, as she had heard all of that before. "I know. It's just…this scene brought up something. A memory I don't like dealing with."

"The bureau has exceptional therapists to help agents process through things like this. So never think you're alone or that something like this makes you less of an agent."

"Thanks," Chloe said, finally managing to stand upright again.

She realized that she suddenly missed her sister very badly. As morbid as it seemed, fond thoughts of Danielle would flood through her whenever memories of the day their mother died surfaced in her head. It was no different now; Chloe could not help but think of her sister. Danielle had been through a lot over the years—a victim of circumstance as well as her own poor decisions. And now that Chloe lived so close, it seemed unthinkable that they should remain so distant.

Sure, she'd invited Danielle to the block part this weekend, but Chloe found herself unable to wait that long. And Chloe suspected that she wouldn't even come.

Suddenly, she knew: she had to see her now.

***

Chloe didn't know why she was so nervous when she knocked on Danielle's door. She knew Danielle was in; the same car she'd had as a teenager was parked in the apartment complex parking lot, still boasting the band stickers. Nine Inch Nails. KMFDM. Ministry. Seeing the car and those stickers brought a pang of nostalgia that was more sadness than anything else.

Has she really not grown up at all? Chloe wondered.

When Danielle answered the door, Chloe saw that she had not. Or, rather, it did not look like it in terms of appearance.

The sisters looked at one another for a period of two seconds before they finally moved in for a brief hug. Chloe saw that Danielle still dyed her hair black. She was also still sporting the lip ring, protruding from the left corner of her mouth. She was wearing a slight bit of black eyeliner and was decked out in a Bauhaus T-shirt and ripped jeans.

"Chloe," Danielle said, breaking into the faintest of smiles. "How have you been?"

It was as if they had seen one another just the day before. That was fine, though. Chloe had not exactly been expecting any sentiment from her sister.

Chloe stepped into the apartment and, not caring much how Danielle would receive it, gave her sister another hug. It had been a little over a year since they had seen one another—and about three since they had actually embraced one another like this. Something about the fact that they now lived in the same city seemed to have bonded something between them—it was something Chloe could feel, something she knew would not need to be vocalized.

Danielle returned the hug, albeit lazily. "So…you're…what?" Danielle teased.

"I'm good," Chloe said. "I know I should have called but…I don't know. I was afraid you'd find some excuse for me not to come by."

"I might have," Danielle admitted. "But now that you're here, come on in. Excuse the mess. Well, actually don't excuse it. You know I've always been messy."

Chloe laughed and when she entered the apartment she was surprised to find the place relatively tidy. The living area was sparsely furnished, just a couch, a TV and TV stand, a coffee table, and a lamp. Chloe knew the rest of the place would be the same. Danielle was the sort of person who lived on only the minimal amount of belongings. The exception, if she hadn't changed since her teen years (and it seemed she hadn't) was music and books. It made Chloe nearly feel guilty for the spacious and elaborate home she had recently purchased with Steven.

"Want me to put on some coffee?" Danielle asked.

"Yeah, that would be great."

They walked into the kitchen, again only boasting the necessities. The table was clearly something that had been scoured from a yard sale, given at least a bit of dignity with a ruffled tablecloth. Two lonely chairs sat at it, one on either side.

"Are you here to bully me about your block party?" Danielle asked.

"Not at all," Chloe said. "I was interning today and came to this crime scene that...well, it brought everything racing back."

"Ouch."

Silence hung between them as Danielle set the coffeemaker up. Chloe watched as her sister moved about the kitchen, a bit creeped out at how much it seemed she had not changed. She could very well be looking at the seventeen-year-old girl who had left home with the hopes of starting a band, despite their grandparents' wishes. Everything looked the same, right down to the sleepy expression.

"Have you heard anything about Dad lately?" Chloe asked.

Danielle only shook her head. "With your job, I thought you'd be the one to hear anything. If there was anything to hear."

"I stopped checking a while ago."

"Cheers to that," Danielle said, covering a small yawn with the back of her hand.

"You look tired," Chloe said.

"I am. Only, not like *sleepy* tired. The doctor had me on these mood stabilizers. It screwed with my sleep. And when you're a bartender who usually doesn't get home until after three in the morning, the last thing you need is a medicine that fucks with your sleep."

"You said the doc *had* you on them. Are you not taking them anymore?"

"No. They were fucking with my sleep, my appetite, and my libido. Ever since I stopped, I feel much better...just tired all the time."

"Why were they prescribed in the first place?" Chloe asked.

"To deal with my nosy sister," Danielle said, only half-joking. She waited a beat before giving an honest answer. "I was starting to get easily depressed. And it would come out of nowhere. I dealt with it in some...pretty dumb ways. Drinking. Sex. *Fixer Upper*."

"If it was for depression, you should probably get back on them," Chloe said, realizing as she said it just how intrusive she was being. "What do you need a libido for anyway?" she asked with a snicker.

22

"For those of us that *aren't* about to get married, they're pretty important. We can't just roll over in bed and get laid whenever we want."

"You never had problems getting guys before," Chloe pointed out.

"And I still don't," she said, bringing mugs of coffee to the table. "It's just too much work. Especially lately. This new one. A serious guy. We decided to take it slow…whatever."

"That's the only reason I'm marrying Steven, you know," Chloe said, trying to get into the joking mood right along with her. "I got tired of having to go out and work for sex."

They both had a laugh at this. It should have felt natural to laugh and smile together again but something about it felt forced.

"So what's up, sis?" Danielle asked. "It's not like you to drop by. Not that I'd know, as we haven't had that opportunity in almost two years."

Chloe nodded, remembering the one time they had actually spent together in the last handful of years. Danielle had been in Philly for some concert and had crashed at her apartment. They'd talked a bit, but not much. Danielle had been hammered and passed out on her couch. Their mom had come up in the conversation, as had their dad. It was the only time Chloe had ever heard Danielle openly speak about wanting to go visit him.

"That scene this morning," Chloe said. "It made me think of that morning outside of the apartment. I kept thinking about the blood at the bottom of the stairs and it got to me. I thought I was going to puke. And I'm *not* that kind of person, you know? The scene itself was pretty vanilla compared to some of the stuff I've seen. It just hit me hard. It made me think of you and I had to see you. Does that make sense?"

"Yeah. The mood stabilizers…I'm pretty sure all of the depression was coming from nightmares I was having about Mom and Dad. I'd have them and then be in a funk for days. Like, not wanting to get out of bed because I trusted no one else out in the world."

"Well, I was going to ask how you cope with it when you think of what happened, but I guess I know the answer, huh?"

Danielle nodded and looked away. "Meds."

"You okay?"

Danielle shrugged but she may as well have flipped Chloe her middle finger. "We're together for about ten minutes and you already go there. God, Chloe…haven't you learned to live your life

23

without dragging that shit up? If you recall, when you called to tell me that you were moving to Pinecrest, we decided to not talk about it. Water under the bridge, remember?"

Chloe was taken aback. She'd just watched Danielle go from dry and sarcastic to absolute furious in the blink of an eye. Sure, the topic of their parents was a sore subject, but Danielle's reaction was bipolar in nature.

"How long have you been off the meds?" Chloe asked.

"Fuck you."

"How long?"

"Three weeks, give or take a few days. Why?"

"Because I've only been here for about fifteen minutes and I can already tell that you need them."

"Thanks, doc."

"Will you start taking them, please? I want you at my wedding. Maid of honor, remember? As selfish as it might seem, I'd like for you to actually enjoy it. So would you please just start taking them again?"

The mention of maid of honor did something to Danielle. She sighed and then relaxed her posture. She was able to look at Chloe again and while she was still angry, there was something warm there as well.

"Fine," she said.

She got up from the table and went to a little decorative wicker basket on the kitchen counter. She pulled out a prescription bottle, shook out a pill, and swallowed it down with her coffee.

"Thank you," Chloe said. She then pressed a bit more, sensing something else amiss. "Is everything else okay?"

Danielle thought about it for a moment and Chloe caught her casting a quick glance toward her apartment door. It was very brief but there was fear there—Chloe was sure of it.

"No, I'm good."

Chloe knew her sister well enough to know not to press it.

"So, what the hell is a block party, anyway?" Danielle asked.

Chloe laughed; she had nearly forgotten Danielle's ability to drop a subject and start another one with all the grace of an elephant in a china shop. And just like that, the subject was changed. Chloe watched her sister to see if she ever looked back to the door with that bit of fear in her eyes, but it never happened again.

Still, Chloe felt that there was something there. Maybe after some time together, Danielle would fess up.

But to what? Chloe wondered, casting a glance at the front door herself.

And it was then that she realized that she really didn't know her sister at all. There were parts of her that seemed very much like the gothed-out seventeen-year-old she'd last known so well. But there was something new to Danielle now…something darker. Something that needed meds to control her moods, to help her sleep and function.

It occurred to Chloe in that moment that she was scared for her sister and she wanted to help in any way she could.

Even if it meant digging into the past.

But not now. Maybe after the wedding. God only knew what sort of arguments and mood swings talking about the death of their mother and incarceration of their father would bring up. Still, Chloe felt the ghosts of her past stronger than ever while sitting there with Danielle and it made her wonder just how haunted Danielle had been by it all.

What kind of ghosts lurked around in Danielle's head? And what, exactly, were they telling her?

She sensed, the way she did a coming storm, that whatever Danielle was suppressing, it would all eventually involve her. Her new life. Her new fiancé, her new house. Her new life.

And it would all lead to nothing good.

CHAPTER FIVE

Danielle sat on her couch, reclining back against Martin, her leg draped over his, and she was very aware that she was not wearing underwear beneath her pajama shorts. Not that it would matter; somehow, he had refused her last night, despite no bra and the skimpy little panties. It seemed Martin was taking this whole taking-things-slow thing seriously.

She was also beginning to think that he was either just being a gentleman or was not sexually attracted to her. The latter was hard to believe, though, because she'd literally felt the proof of his attraction grinding against her legs and hips on the multiple occasions they'd made out.

She tried not to let it bother her. While she was indeed sexually frustrated, there was something to be said about finally finding a man who wanted more than just sex.

Tonight was a great example. They'd chosen to remain low-key, just sitting around her apartment and watching a movie. Beforehand, they had discussed Martin's day. Yet as an assistant manager at a print shop, there were only so many details to discuss. It was like listening to someone explain how paint dried. As for Danielle, she hated talking about her day. As a bartender at a local restaurant, her days were boring. She sat around and read most of the time. The nights were filled with stories to share but by the time she managed to get some sleep and woke up around one in the afternoon, she never wanted to go over them.

Once the niceties were over, they *had* kissed a bit, but it was all very PG. Again, Danielle found that she had no problem with that. Besides, ever since Chloe's visit, she had been bummed out. The mood stabilizers likely wouldn't even kick in until she took her second pill right before bedtime.

Thanks to Chloe's visit, Danielle had been thinking about her mother, her father, and the childhood that had passed her by like a warped flicker of film. Really, all she wanted was to be held by Martin—something it pained her to admit to herself.

They'd settled on one of her DVDs, popping in *The Shawshank Redemption* and curling up together on the couch like a couple of nervous and inexperienced middle school kids. On a few occasions, his hand would slip a little lower than her shoulder and she wondered if he was trying to make a move. But he remained respectable, which was both refreshing and infuriating all at once.

She also noticed that on a few occasions, his phone would ding. It was sitting on her coffee table right in front of them but he elected not to check it. At first, she assumed he was just being polite and not infringing on their date time. But after a while—what Danielle assumed had been at least seven or eight little dings—it started to get obnoxious.

Just as Tim Robbins locked himself in the warden's office and played some opera music over the PA for the prisoners of Shawshank Prison, it dinged one more time. Danielle looked to the phone and then to Martin.

"Are you going to check on that?" she asked. "Someone must really need you for something."

"Nah, it'll be okay," he said. He pulled her closer and stretched out. They were lying side by side. If she wanted, she could easily kiss his neck. She looked at the exposed space there and thought about it. She wondered how he might react if she kissed him there, maybe softly ran her tongue along the side of his neck.

The phone dinged again. Danielle let out a little chuckle and, without any kind of warning, sprang across Martin's chest. She grabbed the phone and pulled it to her chest. Stalled at his lock screen, she said, "What's your pass—"

Martin violently yanked the phone away from her. He looked more surprised than furious. "What was that about?" he asked.

"Nothing," she said. "Just playing around. You can check your phone while you're with me. I don't mind. If it's another girlfriend or something, though, I might have to go bitch-mode on her."

"I don't need you to oversee my phone usage," he snapped.

"Um, hold on. There's no need to get crazy about it. I was just playing around."

He sneered at her and shoved the phone in his pocket. He sighed and sat up, apparently no longer interested in cuddling with her.

"Ah, you're one of those guys, then," she said, still trying to find the line between joking around and being a little persistent. "Guard your phone like it was your dick or something."

"Leave it alone," he said. "Don't be weird about it."

"Me? Martin, I thought you were going to break my wrists getting it out of my hands."

"Well, it's not your phone now, is it? Don't you trust me?"

"I don't know," she said, raising her voice. "We haven't been going out all that long. God, there's no need to get so fucking defensive."

He rolled his eyes at her and looked at the TV. It was a dismissive gesture, one that pissed her off. She shook her head and, doing her best to keep her playful façade front and center, she quickly straddled him. She reached down as if going for his zipper but then angled for the pocket he had put the phone in. With her other hand, she started to tickle his right side.

He was taken aback, clearly unsure how to respond. Yet the moment her fingers found the edge of his phone, he seemed to flip a switch somewhere. He grabbed her arm and pulled it up in a vise-like grip. He then shoved her down on the couch, not yet letting go of her arm. It hurt like hell but she was not about to let him hear her scream out in pain. The speed and strength he showed reminded her that he had once trained to be an amateur boxer.

"Whoa, let go of my fucking arm!"

He did, looking down at her in surprise. The look on his face made her think he had not intended to get that rough with her. He had surprised even himself. But he was also angry; the furrowed brow and trembling shoulders were evidence of that.

"I'm going to go," he said.

"Yeah, good idea," Danielle said. "And don't even bother calling again unless it's going to start with an apology."

He shook his head—whether at himself and his actions or at her, Danielle wasn't sure. She watched him quickly walk for the door, closing it firmly behind him. Danielle sat on the couch, looking toward the door for several moments as she tried to figure out what exactly had happened.

No interest in screwing me and *a surprise temper on him,* she thought. *That dude might be more trouble than he's worth.*

Of course, she'd always been drawn to that kind of man.

She looked at her arm and saw red splotches where he had grabbed her and shoved her down. She was pretty sure they'd bruise. It wouldn't be the first time a guy had put bruises on her but she had really not seen it coming from Martin.

She toyed with the idea of chasing after him to see what had gotten into him. But instead, she stayed on the couch and watched the movie. If her past had taught her anything, it was that men simply weren't worth chasing after. Not even the ones who seemed too good to be true.

She finished the movie by herself and called it a night. As she shut off all the light, she felt like she was being watched—like she was not alone. She knew this was ridiculous, of course, but still could not help but look back to her front door, where the letter had appeared yesterday—and several times before—as if out of nowhere.

She remained on the couch and watched the door, almost expecting another letter to slide through the bottom. And twenty minutes later, when she got up and started getting ready for work, she did so with every light in the apartment on.

Slowly, a creeping paranoia churned within her. It was a familiar one, a feeling that had become something like a close friend over the years—a very close friend ever since those letters started arriving.

She thought of the pills and wondered for a moment if this were all in her head. Everything. Including the letters.

Was any of this real?

She couldn't help reaching back into her past, reminding herself of the darkness she thought she had escaped.

Was she losing her mind again?

CHAPTER SIX

Chloe sat in the waiting room, looking at the sparse reading selection on the coffee table. She had visited two different therapists following her mother's death but had not really understood the purpose of those visits. Now, though, at the age of twenty-seven, she knew why she was here. She had taken Greene's advice and called the on-hand bureau therapist to talk out her reaction to yesterday's crime scene. Now she found herself trying to recall the offices she had visited as child.

"Ms. Fine?" a woman called from the other side of the room.

Chloe had been so deep in her own thoughts that she hadn't heard the door to the waiting room open. A pleasant-looking woman waved her back. Chloe got to her feet and tried her best not to feel like a failure as she followed the woman down a hallway and toward a large office space.

She thought back to what Greene had told her yesterday as they had shared coffee. It was still bright and shining in her mind because it had been the first bit of real advice a seasoned agent had ever given her during her very young career.

"I saw this therapist several times my first year. My fourth crime scene was a murder-suicide. Four bodies in all. One was a three-year-old kid. Rattled the hell out of me. So I can tell you without hesitation…therapy works. Especially if you start it at this stage of your career. I've seen agents think they're hot shit and don't need the help. Don't be one of those, Fine."

So no…needing a therapist did not make her a failure. If anything, she hoped it might make her stronger.

She entered the office and saw an older gentleman of about sixty or so sitting behind a large desk. A window behind the desk revealed a small topiary outside, butterflies darting to and fro. His name was Donald Skinner, and he had been doing this for more than thirty years. She knew this because she had Googled him before deciding to make the appointment. Skinner was very prim and proper; he seemed to expand slightly, filling the room a bit more as he walked over to greet her.

He gestured toward a comfortable-looking armchair in the center of the room. "Please," he said. "Make yourself comfortable."

30

She sat down, clearly nervous. She knew she was probably trying a bit too hard to try to hide it.

"Ever done this before?" Skinner asked.

"When I was much younger," she said.

He nodded as he took a seat in an identical chair positioned in front of hers. When he sat, he hefted his right knee up on his right leg and folded his hands atop them.

"Ms. Fine, why don't you tell me about yourself…ending with why you are here today."

"How far back?" she asked, meaning it as a joke.

"For now, let's just focus on the crime scene yesterday," Skinner answered.

Chloe took a moment to think and then started. She held nothing back, even delving back into her past a bit to paint that picture for him as well. Skinner listened intently and now mulled over everything he had just been told.

"Tell me," Skinner said. "So far, out of the crime scenes you've visited, was this the grisliest?"

"No. But it was the grisliest thing I'd been allowed to actually *see*."

"So you are willing to fully admit that it was this event from your past that caused you to react the way you did?"

"I suppose. I mean, it's never happened before. And even when it sort if *tries* to bother me, I can stomp it out pretty easily."

"I see. Now, are there any other factors that might have come into play? It's a new city. A new instructor, a new house. There's a lot of change."

"My twin sister," Chloe said. "She lives here in Pinecrest. I figured maybe the idea of seeing her again after a year or so…maybe that did it in addition to the scene being so similar."

"That could very well be the case," Skinner asked. "Please forgive me asking such a simple question, but did the murder of your mother lead you to a career with the FBI?"

"Yes. I knew by the time I was twelve, this is what I wanted to do."

"And what about your sister? What does she do?"

"She's a bartender. I think she enjoys it because she only has to be social for a few hours of the day and then she can go home and sleep until noon."

"And does she remember that day the same way you do? Have you spoken about it?"

"We have, but she won't go into great detail. When I try, she shuts me down pretty much right away."

"So go into those details with me right now," Skinner said. "It's clear you need to discuss it somehow. So why not with me...an impartial party?"

"Well, like I said earlier, it seemed like a pretty basic yet unfortunate accident."

"Yet your father was arrested for it," Skinner pointed out. "So to me, as someone not familiar with the case, I don't lean towards accident. It makes me curious how you can see it so clearly as such. So let's go over it. What happened that day? What do you remember?"

"Well, it was an accident *caused* by my father. That's why he was arrested. He didn't even lie about it. He was drunk, Mom made him mad, and he pushed her."

"I've given you the chance to go into greater detail and that's all I'm getting?" Skinner asked in a friendly tone.

"Well, some of it is blurry," Chloe admitted. "You know how past memories are sort of fogged over with rose-colored glasses?"

"Indeed. So...I want to try something with you. Because this is the first time we've met, I'm not going to try hypnosis. I *am* going to try a proven form of therapy, though. It's what some refer to as timeline therapy. For today, I hope it might help to dig further details from that day—details that are right there in your mind but have sort of been tucked away because you're afraid to see them. If you continue to see me, this sort of therapy will eventually help us to pluck the fear and anxiety that arise in you whenever you're faced with that day. Does that sound like something you'd be willing to undergo today?"

"Yes," she said without hesitation.

"Okay. Good. So...let's begin with where you were sitting. I want you to close your eyes and relax. Take a moment or two to clear your head and get comfortable. Give me a tiny nod when you are ready."

Chloe did as she was asked. She allowed herself to sink back into the chair. It was a very comfortable faux leather armchair. She felt that she was still tensing her shoulders, uncomfortable with being so vulnerable in front of someone she had never met. She sighed deeply and felt her shoulders go limp. She nestled into the chair and listened for the hum of the air conditioner. She found it, listened to its droning, and then gave a nod. She was ready.

"Okay," Skinner said. "Out on that stoop with your sister. Now, even if you can't remember the sort of shoes you were wearing that day, I want you to imagine that you are looking at your feet. Look down at your shoes. I want you to focus on them and nothing else— just the shoes you were wearing that day when you were ten years old. You and your sister out on the stoop. But keep your eyes only on those shoes. Describe them to me."

"Chuck Taylors," Chloe said. "Red. Scuffed up. Big floppy laces."

"Perfect. Now study the laces. Really zone in on them. Then I want your ten-year-old self to stand up without looking away from those laces. I want you to stand up and walk back to where you were before discovering the blood on the carpet at the bottom of the stairs. I need you to go back a few hours. But don't look away from those laces. Can you do that?"

Chloe knew she was not hypnotized but the instructions seemed so simple. So basic and easy. She stood up inside her mind and walked back into the apartment. When she did, she saw the blood, saw her mother.

"Mom is right there at the bottom of the stairs," she said. "Lots of blood. Danielle is somewhere, crying. Dad is pacing."

"Okay. But just look at your shoelaces," Skinner instructed. "And then see if you can go back farther. Can you do that?"

"Yeah. Easy. I'm with Beth…a friend of mine. We just got back from a movie. Her mom took us. She dropped me off and stayed there on the curb until I got inside. She always did that, not pulling away until she saw me go inside."

"Okay. So watch those shoelaces as you get out of the car and walk up the stairs. Then take me through the rest of the afternoon."

"I went inside the building and then up to the second floor, where our apartment was. When I walked to the door and pulled out the keys to unlock it, I hear Dad inside. So I just walked in. I closed the door and headed for the living room but saw Mom's body. It was at the bottom of the stairs. Her right arm was pinned beneath her. Her nose looked all smashed up and there was blood everywhere. Most of her face was covered with it. It was all over the carpet, right there at the bottom of the stairs. I think Dad might have tried to move the body…"

Chloe trailed off here. She was finding it hard to focus on those ratty old shoelaces. She knew the scene she was relaying far too well to ignore it.

"Danielle is standing right there, right over her. She has some blood on her hands and her clothes. Dad is talking really loudly into the phone, telling someone to come quickly, there's been an accident. When he gets off, he looks at me and starts crying. He threw the phone across the room and it shattered against the wall. He came over to us and hunkered down. He said he was sorry…he said there was an ambulance on the way. He then looked at Danielle and we could barely understand him through the tears. He said Danielle needed to go upstairs. She needed to change her clothes.

"She did, and I followed her. I asked her what had happened but she wouldn't talk to me. She wouldn't even cry. Eventually, we started to hear sirens. We sat there with Dad, waiting for him to tell us what would happen next. But he never did. The ambulance arrived, then the police. A friendly policeman took us outside on the stoop and stayed there with us until Dad was brought out in handcuffs. Until they brought Mom's body out…"

Suddenly, the vision of the busted up shoelaces was gone. She was back on the stoop, waiting for her grandmother to pick them up. The overweight cop was with her and although she didn't know him, he made her feel safe.

"You okay?" Skinner asked.

"Yeah," she said with a nervous smile. "The part about Dad throwing the phone…I had totally forgotten about that."

"How's the remembered sight of it make you feel?"

It was a hard question to answer. Her father had always been quick to temper but seeing him do it in the wake of what had happened to her mother almost made him seem weak and vulnerable.

"It makes me feel sad for him."

"Have you blamed him for your mother's death ever since it happened?" Skinner asked.

"It honestly just depends on the day. Depends on my mood."

Skinner nodded and broke his statue-like posture. He got to his feet and looked down at her with a reassuring smile.

"I think we're good for today. Please call me if you experience this sort of reaction to a crime scene again. And I would like to see you again soon. Can we set up an appointment?"

Chloe thought about it and nodded. "We can, but I have a wedding coming up soon and we have all these meetings with florists and bakers…it's a nightmare. Can I call you with a date?"

"Of course. And until then…stick closely to Agent Greene. He's a good man. And he was right to direct you to me. Please know that this early in your career, having to come to someone like me to deal with your issues means nothing. It is not a reflection of your talents."

Chloe nodded. She knew this but it was still nice to hear Skinner say it. She got up and thanked him for his time. As she walked out the door and into the waiting room, she saw her father throwing the phone. But then there was a comment he'd made—one she had not forgotten but had become muddied until today.

He had looked at Danielle and, with something far too close to urgency in his voice, had said: "Danielle, honey...go change your clothes. There's not much time before they get here."

That comment rolled through Chloe's head for most of the remainder of the afternoon, chilling her while also poking at a locked door she had managed to ignore for the last seventeen years.

CHAPTER SEVEN

Danielle woke up at eight o'clock, feeling as if she had not slept well at all. She'd gotten in from work at 2:45 and collapsed into bed at 3:10. She usually had no problem sleeping until well after eleven—sometimes even later—but when her eyes opened at 8:01 that morning, she could not go back to sleep. Truth be told, she really hadn't slept very well ever since she'd known that Chloe was coming back into town. It had felt like her past was slowly following her and it would not stop until it swallowed her whole.

Cranky and tired, Danielle showered and then ate breakfast. She did it all with Skinny Puppy's *Too Dark Park* album playing in the background. As she placed her breakfast dishes in the sink, she realized she'd have to go grocery shopping today. Most days, this did not bother her. But there was the occasional day where she felt like going out into public was a mistake...that people were watching her, waiting for her to fuck something up and point fingers.

She also feared that any time she went out allowed the letter writer a chance to follow her. One of these days, she figured the writer would stop playing around with her and just kill her.

Maybe today would be that day.

She drove to the grocery store, already knowing full well that this was going to be one of those days...one of those days where she was going to be afraid of everything. One of those days where she would constantly be looking over her shoulder. She drove quickly, even running a red light along the way, wanting to get the trip over.

Ever since Danielle started receiving the disturbing notes under her door, she found it anxiety-inducing to be in a public place for very long. It was far too easy to imagine the person who had been writing those letters to be following her. Even at work, she wondered if the writer was sitting at the bar, having just received a drink from her. When she picked up her Chinese food, was he following her, waiting to finally jump her as she walked back to her car?

Even after she had arrived safely at her destination, hurrying into the grocery store and practically racing a cart with a squeaky wheel down the aisle, the worry was there. The letter writer could be there with her, mirroring her steps on the next aisle over, maybe getting a good look at her across the produce section or across the cereal aisle.

It was a very real fear that flashed through her head the day following the surprising turn of events with Martin. The paranoia sank into her, causing her to lower her head and push up her shoulders. If someone wanted to see her face, they'd need to be very purposeful about it, to the point of stopping her and hunching down.

She hated that she was like this. She'd always faced these kinds of issues, which was why most of her dating relationships rarely lasted more than a month. She knew she'd developed a reputation for being a bit of a slut during her first tenure here in Pinecrest, but it hadn't been because she enjoyed sleeping around. It was just that by the time she was comfortable enough with a guy to sleep with him, she'd start to assume the worst about him. She'd end the relationship, take some time to recover, and then start again.

She'd gotten a bit better when she'd moved back to Pinecrest a few years ago. She'd left Boston and felt like she was retreating…but that was okay. She was at least retreating to somewhere familiar. The hardest thing to get used to was the stagnant dating scene. It had been okay at first, although she'd managed to ruin every single relationship she'd started. That's why the fight with Martin had struck her so hard.

Of course, there was the downside to Pinecrest. Far too many people remembered her and Chloe. They remembered how the poor little Fine girls had ended up living with their grandparents after their mother had died and their father had been taken to prison.

"Danielle, is that you?"

She turned toward the voice, startled. She'd been so lost in her thoughts that she'd managed to fully expose her face while reaching up for a box of Froot Loops. She found herself looking at a face from her past—a woman who looked terribly familiar but whom she couldn't quite place.

"Do you not remember me?" the woman asked, on the verge of entertained and offended. She was probably forty-five, maybe fifty. And no, Danielle did not remember this woman.

"I guess you *don't* remember me," the woman said. "I guess you were only thirteen or fourteen the last time I saw you. I'm Tammy Wyler. I was a friend of your mom's."

37

"Oh yeah, sure," Danielle said. She did not remember the woman at all but the name did sound familiar. Danielle assumed she was one of the family friends who had visited her grandparents in the year or two following the death of her mother.

"I almost didn't recognize you," Tammy said. "Your hair is...darker."

"Yeah," Danielle said unenthusiastically. She supposed the last time Tammy Wyler had seen her, she'd only just started her full rebellion mode. Back then, at thirteen or fourteen years of age, she'd usually opted for neon pink hair with black stripes. Now it was raven black, a style she realized was old and used up but seemed to still fit her perfectly.

"I always knew you came back around here but well...I don't know. I just never really got around to looking you up after you moved. You went to Boston or something for a while, right?"

"Right."

"Oh, so I hear Chloe is back in town, too. Bought a new house out near Lavender Hills, right?"

"Yeah, she's back," Danielle said, quickly approaching her tolerance limit for small talk and bullshit.

"I heard through the grapevine that she lives just a few houses away from a girl you guys went to high school with. I actually live about two streets over from her."

Poor Chloe, Danielle thought.

"Oh, and did she tell you about the block party?" Tammy asked, apparently unable to keep her mouth shut for any more than three seconds at a time.

"She did," Danielle said. She was hoping Tammy would take her short responses as a cue that she really wasn't the sort to just chat it up in the aisle of the grocery store.

There was a brief silence between the two of them where Tammy *did* seem to piece this together. She looked around awkwardly and bowed out with as much grace as she could. "Well, I hope you can make it. It was good running into you, Danielle."

"Yeah, you too," Danielle said.

She wasted no time in hunching her shoulders and casting her head down as she pushed her cart farther down the cereal aisle. Her need to get out of the store and back to her apartment was stronger than ever—now not just because of her usual paranoid feelings, but because of the awkward encounter with Tammy Wyler.

She rushed through the rest of her shopping, nearly colliding with an elderly lady in the dairy section. She went through the self-checkout (because why deal with chatty cashiers if you didn't have to) and hurried out to her car. When she was back out in the fresh air, she felt a little better. Of course, maybe the man sending the letters was sitting in one of the cars in the parking lot. Maybe he had been following her in the grocery store, listening to her speak awkwardly to Tammy.

She put her bags in the back seat and started the car. Before she had a chance to back out of her parking spot, her phone rang. She saw Martin's name on the display and didn't hesitate to answer. If he was calling to argue, she was game. If he was calling to apologize, she'd be open to that, too. Truth be told, she just liked the idea of being on the phone with someone she knew in that moment.

She answered with a simple, "Hey."

"Hey, Danielle," Martin said. "Look, I owe you one hell of an apology for last night. And not for just for getting rough. I shouldn't have been so weird about my phone. It's just that things are sort of going to hell at work. That's what the texts were. I knew it the moment they started coming in. I didn't want to face it last night. Does that make sense?"

"It does. But what doesn't make sense is why you didn't just tell me that last night."

"Because I'm stupid," he said. "I didn't want you to know that my job might very well be on the chopping block. And then when you got really playful about it, I just took it the wrong way. Danielle...I have never hurt a woman. Please believe me on that. And putting my hands on you like that last night...God, I'm so sorry."

She said nothing. Her arms had bruised up a bit and she *had* felt a bit in danger. Still, she could hear what she thought was genuine sadness in his voice.

"Danielle?"

"I'm here," she said. "Just...I wish you would have told me all of this before it got to the point it did."

"I know. Please...can you forgive me?"

She knew she would. She was simply trying to think of what she could do to turn things in her favor. She smiled at the idea that came to her and couldn't help herself.

"Well, this PG relationship is coming to a stop. You're going to meet me at my apartment tonight and we're going to make out. I'm not going to sleep with you yet but...well, there's going to be touching."

"Um...okay. I can do that," he said, clearly confused yet appreciative.

"That's not it. My sister just moved into town. I told you that, right?"

"Yeah."

"Well, it's some swanky uptight neighborhood. The kind that has block parties. She's invited me to a block party this weekend. I want you to come with me."

"Oh. Okay. I can do that."

"Good," she said. "I'll see you tonight, then."

She ended the call just like that. She liked the idea that he had no idea how to respond to her. She also liked that she basically had control of him now—not in any sort of devious way, but just so that she could feel a little more comfortable around him.

Feeling a bit better, the paranoia now just a little seed of worry in the back of her head, she headed home. And she was delighted to find that she was excited for tonight. It had been a very long time since she'd actually *wanted* a man's hands on her.

That, plus the quickly fading paranoia, made her wonder if maybe Martin might be the right man for her after all. He seemed to be changing all sorts of things about her. Of course, he knew very little about those things and she'd keep it that way for as long as she could.

She continued home, starting to wonder just what in the hell you were supposed to wear to a block party.

It was almost enough to drive away the spike of paranoia that had firmly latched itself into her earlier that morning and had remained on her in the grocery store.

Almost.

She grabbed her phone and dialed up Chloe. She didn't even allow her sister time to say *Hello* before she started speaking.

"This block party....can I bring a date?"

"...Yes, of course," Chloe said, clearly stunned.

"I'll see you tomorrow, then."

And with that, she hung up the phone, wondering what the hell she had just gotten herself into.

CHAPTER EIGHT

Chloe was pruning a head of broccoli when the doorbell rang. She knew right away that it was Danielle. She was quite nervous about this but, at the same time, happy to see something as stable as an actual boyfriend in her sister's life. Steven, meanwhile, was skeptical. He figured the boyfriend would be someone just like Danielle, creating an even tenser environment with two people to worry about.

Chloe had managed to shrug off Steven's attitude toward Danielle for most of their four years together but now that the wedding was getting closer, it was really starting to annoy her. But that was an argument for another day.

Chloe wiped her hands off on a dish towel and walked to the door. She took a steadying breath before she answered it. She hated to sway toward Steven's line of thinking but she was slightly worried about what Danielle would look like.

When she answered the door and found her sister somewhat made up and striking, she nearly did a double take. The black hair was put up into a cute little bun in the back. She was wearing a slight bit of makeup—just enough to help her cheeks glow—and had thankfully decided against band T-shirts or her standard pseudo-goth look. She *was* wearing black, but it was a semi-dressy tank top with delicate straps. Her tattoo showed along her upper back but that wasn't too distracting. The jeans she wore surprised Chloe the most; they were basic dark denim and quite tight, showing off her curves in a way Chloe had never seen before.

"Danielle, you look amazing," Chloe said.

"Yeah, don't get used to it." She stepped aside and nodded to the man who had come with her. "This is Martin."

"Pleased to meet you," Martin said, extending his hand.

Chloe shook it and noticed for the first time that he was dressed basically how she'd expected Danielle to show up. His T-shirt was wrinkled and his cargo shorts had a noticeable tear underneath one of the pockets. He wore a tattered pair of flip-flops with well-worn bands. His hair looked like it hadn't been washed in a few days. He looked tired and out of sorts. Chloe couldn't help but wonder if he was high. And if not high, almost certainly a user. She dreaded the moment when Steven met him.

"This house is enormous," Danielle said as she stepped through the foyer and into the living room.

"Yeah, it does feel big," Chloe said. "We're nearly unpacked. I think once all the crap is out of the boxes, it might not feel so big."

The sunlight was reflecting off of the polished hardwood floors as she led Danielle and Martin into the kitchen. Chloe bit back a tiny smile, enjoying the feeling of sort of showing off in front of Danielle. There was no malice in the feeling, but more of a basic sense of pride.

"Got kids?" Martin asked.

Wow, Danielle really doesn't talk about me, Chloe thought. "No," she answered. "Not yet and no time soon."

"Then why all the empty space?" Martin asked.

She was taken off guard by the nearly rude question but kept her cool. "Because you never know. We may have one someday, and we may have five."

"Whoa," Steven said as he came in through the door that connected the kitchen and the back deck. "Five?"

"You never know," Chloe said with a smirk.

"Oh, I'm pretty sure," Steven said. He then looked at Danielle and was genuinely taken off guard. "Danielle, you look great!"

"Thanks, Steven. Steven, this is Martin," she said, making introductions.

"Yeah, nice to meet you," Steven said. Chloe could tell that he had already judged Martin based on his appearance. And that was fine with her; she'd basically done the same thing, too.

"Based on what I know about Danielle," Martin said, "I didn't think her sister would be the block party type."

"Yeah, we were never really the same," Danielle said.

"Oh, that's for sure," Chloe said. "Different at just about every level you can think of."

"And what type did you think her sister would be?" Steven asked, taking an almost defensive stance beside Chloe.

"I don't know, man. Laid back, I guess?"

It was clear Steven had something else to say but had the good sense to bite it back. He nodded briskly to Danielle and said: "Good to see you, Danielle."

With that, he grabbed a beer from the fridge and headed back out onto the deck.

It would figure, Chloe thought. *The one time Danielle decides to be as civil as she knows how to be, her boyfriend turns out to be a prick. And the sad thing is, I don't think he even knows it. Maybe he's as socially awkward as Danielle. Maybe she finally met the right man, the perfect match.*

"So," Danielle said, doing her best to ease the tension, "Chloe, do you remember a really annoying woman named Tammy Wyler?"

Chloe thought about it for a moment and shrugged. She was still working the broccoli as she tried to pin the name. "Sounds familiar. One of Grandma's friends, maybe?"

"One of *Mom's* friends, or so she said. I ran into her in the grocery store today. She knew you had moved here. I think she lives a few streets over. She's coming to the block party, too."

Chloe shook her head with a smile. "Man…I forgot how quickly word travels around a place like this."

The sisters shared a knowing and slightly uncomfortable look, smiling at one another. Martin, meanwhile, looked a little uncomfortable and clearly out of his element. He was looking to the door that led to the back deck, as if wondering what he'd said to piss Steven off.

"So," Chloe said as she dumped the broccoli into a bowl with dressing and other ingredients. "You guys ready for the party?"

"I don't know," Danielle said. "I'm not really well-versed in uppity block parties."

"Just smiling, nodding, and getting drunk, right?" Martin asked.

Chloe forced out a chuckle, deciding that she did not like Martin at all. *Oh God,* she thought. *This was a mistake, wasn't it?*

Maybe it was. But it was too late to go back on it now. All she could do was mix up her broccoli salad and hope for the best.

***

As much as Chloe hated to admit it, she thought Danielle's lack of enthusiasm for the block party was on point. They walked together in a loose little group, Chloe and Steven in the lead with Danielle and Martin close behind. Chloe hadn't been quite sure what to expect, but it wasn't what she was walking through, that was for sure.

The women, for the most part, were dressed in gorgeous sundresses. Not only that, but there were women who were easily pushing fifty who were wearing tight and revealing outfits—

nothing trashy, but enough to catch the eye of any man in the vicinity. There were glasses of wine everywhere, and trendy high-dollar craft beers, which Martin helped himself to right away.

Some people had set up lawn chairs and umbrellas at the foot of their driveway while others had opened up their entire garages for the party. Some people blared Bob Marley from their porches and decks while others opted for Jack Johnson. It was like a little fair right in the middle of the neighborhood.

Danielle quickly stepped up to Chloe, walking by her side. "So this is far too swanky for me. I'm going to take advantage of the free booze and then I think Martin and I are going to split."

"Stop it," Chloe said, hoping Danielle was just trying to be funny. "You haven't even been here for ten minutes."

When she saw Danielle smiling, she was relieved. Danielle was trying—she was *really* trying to not only appease her, but to have fun. Even when they were approached by two different women who recognized them from high school, Danielle did her best to seem social. She wasn't chatty with them—nor did Chloe expect her to be—but she did remain mostly civil.

As they walked through the party and made introductions, Chloe's agent-side took over a bit. Some of these people seemed to live the very definition of privileged upper-class Americans. The wives rolled their eyes at their husbands a lot. A few men and women who passed one another on the arm of someone else shared knowing looks. Chloe couldn't help but wonder how many affairs were actively taking place in Lavender Hills.

But at least it all looks good on the surface, she thought ironically. She sighed and looked over at her sister.

"Thanks for this," Chloe said as they stepped away from the second acquaintance from high school. "I know how difficult and boring it is for you."

"Well, just as long as you know...oh, and also...Tammy Wyler, dead ahead. Twelve o'clock."

Chloe looked ahead and was surprised to find that she *did* recognize the woman who had spotted them and was hurrying over. There were two other women with her, all of whom looked to be middle-aged.

"Beware," Danielle said from behind her. "This woman likes to *taaalk*."

"This is where I hop off the train," Steven whispered in her ear. "There's a lawyer friend of mine over there that I need to catch up with."

Before Chloe could make any kind of abandonment joke, Steven was gone. Danielle and Martin remained by her side. It made Chloe feel stranded while reminding her of just how antisocial Danielle typically was.

Keep it together for just a little while longer, sis. Please…

"Chloe Fine!" Tammy Wyler said as she approached. "My gosh, you've grown up."

"Hi, Mrs. Wyler," Chloe said.

Tammy waved the name away and shook her head. "Gosh, no! Just Tammy, please. So how are you liking the neighborhood?"

"It's nice. Very quiet, very quaint."

"Oh, it's so exciting to have you here. Now, where's this fiancé of yours?"

"He's mingling with some friends. Don't worry—you'll meet him soon enough."

Tammy looked back and forth between Chloe and Danielle, a beaming smile on her face. "Even though the hair is obviously different, you two look so eerily alike," she commented. "My goodness, you both look just like your mother."

"Yes, Grandma always made it a point to tell us that," Chloe said.

Something about Tammy's attitude was off-putting. She was cheerful in the same way Kathleen Saunders was cheerful—almost annoyingly so. But there was something very fake about it, too. She supposed it had to do with Danielle being there. People had never really known how to take Danielle and these older and seemingly snobby women would be no exception. To them, Danielle was likely nothing more than just a scar on the otherwise beautiful face of their generic little neighborhood.

"I was so sorry to hear about your grandmother's passing," Tammy said. "I regret not making it to the funeral but I was in France with my daughter when it happened."

"Oh, that's okay," Danielle said.

"Sort of lovely how it happened so shortly after your grandfather passed, though," Tammy said. "I guess they just couldn't stand to be apart."

"Yeah, it seemed fitting," Chloe said. But she was thinking: *Oh my God, I bet this is eating into Danielle like acid.*

"I thought you should both know that I think of Gale often. We weren't very close—not best friends or anything like that. But we knew each other well enough. She was beautiful and *so* smart. We were in a book club together and the way she pulled things apart...man, everyone rolled their eyes at her. She basically ruled over the Pinecrest Public Library Book Club."

"I remember her being a bit of a bookworm," Chloe said.

"Yeah," Danielle said. "Always had her nose stuck in a book. I used to steal her Danielle Steel books and look for the juicy parts."

Tammy placed an arm around the shoulders of one of the other women who had come over with her. "Girls, I don't know if you remember this lady, but this is Ruthanne Carwile. She and Gale were practically best friends when they were in school."

"Sure were," Ruthanne said. "I even babysat the two of you on more than a few occasions."

As with Tammy, there was something in Ruthanne's look that frustrated Chloe. She could not put her finger on it. It was like these women not only knew their past, but were still using it to form opinions of the Fine sisters. She also hated when people she barely knew talked to her about her mother by using her name. She had never understood why, though.

It was more than just poorly hiding their feelings now. Now it seemed almost mysterious...like they were hiding something. And Ruthanne even looked a little anxious.

"Holy shit!" Danielle exclaimed, out of nowhere. "I remember you! We used to watch cartoons at your house. You had all these videotapes with old cartoons."

"That's right," Ruthanne said, her anxious look replaced with delight. "And you loved Woody Woodpecker."

Martin had a laugh at this. Danielle elbowed him in the ribs and gave him a look that could have sliced through steel.

"I tell you," Ruthanne said. "I know your mother would love to see that the two of you ended up back in the same town. She loved you both so much. Man, I wish you could have seen that woman when she was younger. In her early twenties, she had men tripping over one another for a chance to date her. And *funny*..."

The smile on Chloe's face was genuine. She'd always loved to hear stories about her mother, even the exaggerated ones that their grandmother used to tell. She was about to respond when Steven's hand fell on her shoulder. Without even bothering to wait for a break in the conversation, he interjected himself.

"Hey, babe...come over here. There's someone I want you to meet."

"Hold on. These women knew my mom."

"Oh, this will only take a second."

Two things became abundantly clear to Chloe in that moment. One was something she had already learned somewhat—that whenever Steven wanted something, it was, to him, the most important thing on the planet at that time. The second was that Tammy and Ruthanne were giving Steven side-eyed glances and were embarrassed for her. Which, in turn, embarrassed Chloe.

So she could start a scene and argue or she could excuse herself from these ladies and go with Steven.

As it turned out, she didn't have to do either. There was another factor that she had not even expected, one that made her cringe when it presented itself.

Martin leaned in and whispered something to Danielle. Only Martin was not the best at whispering, apparently. Everyone heard it: Danielle, Chloe, Tammy, Ruthanne, and Steven.

"What, does he think he has her trained like a dog or something?"

Martin seemed to know at once that he had been too loud. Everyone looked at him awkwardly. Tammy and Ruthanne took a step back, looking at one another as if the other had a plan to get out of this awkward situation. Yet he didn't seem to care.

"What the hell did you say?" Steven asked, taking an aggressive step toward him.

Martin did not back up. He simply held his arms up in a show of surrender. A bottle of beer dangled in his left hand. Steven reached out and slapped it away. It shattered on the pavement. The sound of it caught the attention of others who were standing nearby.

When Chloe saw Steven rushing forward, her instinct was to reach out and take his arm. She could easily toss him to the ground. Some of the most basic of her physical training gave her about three different ways to take him down before things escalated. But she stopped when she thought of the embarrassment that would cause him. So instead, she let him go and was helpless for a moment as she watched

"Steven," Chloe hissed. "Stop it."

She'd only seen him this aggressive once before. It had been at an Eagles game in Philly when he nearly got into a fight with someone cursing loudly behind them. Seeing him like that had frightened her a bit but it had also showed her that he was passionate about certain things.

Martin moved so quickly that it took everyone by surprise. He threw a perfectly formed punch, clipping Steven's face, causing him to spin to the right.

47

Martin then grabbed Steven's arm, wrenched it forward, and then expertly applied a headlock. She was shocked when she saw the deadly pressure Martin was applying.

"Steven!" Chloe cried.

"Whoa, wait, Martin…" Danielle said.

Both women rushed to stop the squabble. A few other nearby men were rushing to assist as well. Seeing the fight getting worse and potentially out of hand, Chloe could no longer simply stand by. She had no idea what had gotten into Steven and while she was irritated with Martin, he was a stranger. She thought she knew Steven and, quite frankly, had no idea he was capable of such temper and violence. And right now, he was in a very dangerous situation. She wondered what kind of training Martin had because a random bum off the street would not be capable of moving so quickly and with such poise.

Chloe's training kicked in, and she, with the help of two middle-aged men, managed to haul Martin off of Steven.

The area below Steven's right eye was swelling and his head was flushed and red from the pressure of the headlock. Worse, though, was his look of humiliation.

She then looked at Martin, wanting to assess the damage that had been done. But he looked unharmed.

Embarrassed at Steven's actions, Chloe then looked at her sister. She was worried what this scene might do to their relationship, how it might push them even farther apart.

She saw the slight smile on Danielle's face and something about it jarred her. Had she actually enjoyed watching the fight happen? Had she *liked* watching Steven get bested in front of all of their new neighbors?

"Danielle?" she said softly.

Danielle blinked and looked away from Martin. She met Chloe's eyes and the smile disappeared. Instead, she looked around at the gathered crowd that had come to view the fight and then immediately looked to the ground. Her eyes went blank, her shoulders slumped.

"Come on, Danielle," Martin said as he got to his feet. "These fuckers have had enough of a show for today."

Martin started storming off. Danielle followed slowly behind. She gave Chloe only the slightest glance of acknowledgment as she left. Chloe saw a lot of the scared and shut-off ten-year-old sister she worried so much about when they were kids, after their mom had died. It was like looking directly into the face of a ghost.

And, like any worthwhile ghost, it frightened Chloe quite badly.

"Okay, that's enough," Steven said. "Show's over, everyone."

It then occurred to Chloe that more than fifty people were still watching the scene even as Danielle and Martin walked away. She looked down at the pavement and reached out for Steven's hand, ready to head back home. But he yanked his hand away and stormed off ahead of her.

Chloe did not lift her eyes. She followed after Steven and although she continued to look at the street beneath her feet, she could still feel people's stares on her. And although she hated to admit it, she hated Danielle in that moment...for bringing Martin, for associating with men like him.

But you invited her, she told herself. *You wanted her here. What does that say about you?*

She thought of that smile on Danielle's face. It carried some sort of secret...maybe one that Danielle wasn't even aware of.

And as far as Chloe was concerned, that was the scariest thing of all.

CHAPTER NINE

Chloe entered the front door less than twenty seconds after Steven. She felt tiny darts in her back all the way home from the stares of the people they would have as neighbors for the foreseeable future. When she closed the front door behind her, she saw Steven sitting on the couch, looking at the floor and clenching his fists. He was fuming.

"Talk to me, Steven," Chloe said.

"Who the hell acts like that when you've first met someone?" he asked. "Who acts like that, ever?" When it was clear that Chloe intended to give no answer, he kept going on. "The good news is that your sister found another outcast that's perfect for her. Neither one of them knows how to act when they're around other civilized people. What a joke."

"That's not quite fair," Chloe said. "Danielle at least tried to dress up a bit for today. And if you noticed, she was actually pretty civil."

"Yeah, compared to her usual weird antics and antisocial behavior, she was *charming*."

"Steven, I know you're pissed and maybe you even have a right to be. But Danielle had nothing to do with this."

"Of course she did! She brought him here, didn't she?"

"Yes, she did. But she did not whisper in his ear. She did not ask him to throw that punch, and also—you're the one who knocked the beer bottle out of Martin's hand. Sorry, but you can't blame either of those on her."

"Oh my God, Chloe. Please don't tell me you're taking her side on this."

"I'm taking no one's side. What I *do* need to know is where the hell this violent outburst of yours came from. I've never seen you so angry before. And I've *never* seen you throw a punch. It was scary, Steven."

"I know. I just...you know, as bad as it sounds, I don't care. They were embarrassing me. We have to live around these people, Chloe. This is our life now. And we're here less than a week and your oddball sister and her stupid boyfriend have essentially ruined that for us."

"That's a little overdramatic," Chloe said. "Even for you."

"Oh, is it? Well, while I'm being overdramatic, let me go ahead and tell you this: you need to find a new maid of honor because there's no way in hell I'm letting her anywhere *near* the wedding."

Chloe set her glass of water down and did her best to let her tremors of anger subside. They'd only ever had two serious arguments—a third one currently progressing before her very eyes—but on each of those occasions, she had to remind herself that she was not in a class or interning on a case. She could not grill him in the same way she had sometimes grilled people as part of her training.

"Steven, I'm afraid you have no say in that. She's my sister. She *will* be my maid of honor. You have no say in it. And neither do your overprotective parents."

"I think they *should*," he said. "They are, after all, footing the bill."

Chloe drew in a sharp breath, taking it in as an attempt to keep any harsh words from coming out of her mouth. In the end, she simply picked up the glass of water with her left hand and then showed Steven the middle finger of her right hand. She stormed out of the kitchen and to the back deck. She slammed the door behind her, almost hoping she might break something inside in the process.

She sat down in one of their deck chairs beneath the decorative patio umbrella. As she seethed, she could hear the commotion of the block party on all sides—the murmur of conversation and the occasional outburst of muffled laughter.

Probably talking about how crazy the new family in the neighborhood is, she thought. *Probably laughing about the fight between Steven and Martin.*

"Screw 'em," she said quietly to herself.

But even as she said that, trying to pretend that she did not care, there was one moment from the event that stuck out in her mind. It was that thin and nearly sinister little smile she had caught on Danielle's face.

It was somehow worse than the blank and distant expression she had gotten used to during their teenage years.

Something dark and a little evil seemed to be lurking behind that smile—as if she had enjoyed the fact that Steven and Martin were fighting. As if she had enjoyed the idea of causing chaos in the midst of such a perfect little suburban paradise.

Chloe tried to get the image out of her head but it went nowhere. Instead, she found herself picturing that smile looking out into a crowd from her position as a maid of honor in several weeks.

It was *not* a pretty picture.

She let out a deep sigh as she sank into the chair. She was going to have to talk to Danielle. She was going to have to find out what had been going on in the years since they had last actually spoken and hope the sister she had once known wasn't too far gone.

CHAPTER TEN

Danielle stared out the window of Martin's car, hating the fact that she felt like an angry child giving her parents the silent treatment. She wanted to ask Martin what had driven him to be so obnoxious at Chloe's house and during the block party. He'd always been a little irritating but never to that level. She also didn't ask him because she was pretty sure she knew. He'd acted that way for the same reason Danielle had found it difficult to look Chloe in the eye—for the same reason she always seemed to shrink inside of herself when she was around Steven.

It was because they had stepped into another world today. It was a world they told themselves they hated, a world they didn't need and did not care for. But truth be told, it was a world that Danielle had always dreamed for herself. She was making decent money as a bartender—it all came in the form of tips after eleven o'clock at night, really—and she spent very little money. She knew that one day, if she kept up with such practices, she would be able to afford her own house—maybe not in a neighborhood like Lavender Hills, but something much nicer than her one-bedroom apartment.

While Martin had never come out and said as much, she knew he had similar feelings. Yet today was the first time she'd ever actually seen him in such an environment. Needless to say, it had not gone well.

"That Steven guy is an asshole," Martin said as they neared her apartment. "A little pretentious, don't you think?"

"Yeah, I think that's safe to say." It wasn't a lie, as she had never really cared much for Steven anyway.

"He didn't like me, right from the start," Martin said. "It was obvious."

"That might be true," Danielle said. "But did you really have to make such smart-ass comments?"

"Hey, the one thing I said that set him off, I whispered to you. It's not my fault he heard. What was he doing? Eavesdropping? Just waiting for me to say one thing wrong so he could go off on me in front of all of his snotty new neighbors?"

"I don't know," Danielle said. "But I have to be honest with you. I didn't peg you as one of these guys who had to resort to name-calling and fist fights when something doesn't go your way. At the end of the day...you threw the first punch."

"So sorry to disappoint you," he said.

He slammed his hand down on the steering wheel.

"What is it?" she asked. She wasn't scared of his little mood swings. If anything, she found it entertaining. She could easily remember him getting upset with her the other night, so upset that he had pushed her down on the couch and bruised her arm. But if he did that sort of shit again, she'd be ready...and he'd be sorry.

"Nothing. The gas light is on. We're almost out of gas."

Danielle said nothing. She just looked out the window, wondering how it was that when Martin got angry about something, it fed into everything else about that day—even something as trivial as needing to put gas in the car.

He pulled the car into the next gas station they came to. He had a set expression on his face as he opened the door and stalked his way to the pumps, as if he thought the world was out to get him today. Danielle had never seen him in this sort of a funk and it made her feel like an idiot for thinking he might be this perfect man.

It brought to mind just how protective he had been about his phone the other night. Sure, he told her *later* that it had just been something concerning work. But why hadn't he said something then, when she was trying to be funny about it?

She looked down at the console and saw his phone. She'd spied him earlier putting his code in on the lock screen, so she knew how to get in.

She took a glance out the window and saw that he was zoned out, staring across the street while the gas pumped.

To hell with it, she thought.

She grabbed the phone and quickly punched in the four-digit code. The phone unlocked and she instantly went to his messages. She scrolled through, looking for texts from a couple of days ago. There were texts from her and there *were* texts from work. There were also messages from one of his weirdo friends but then, a few messages down, messages from a number he had not saved—the ID showed only a number and not a name.

She opened it and looked back to see if he was still zoned out. He was. She had a few seconds, at least until the *click* of the pump when the tank was filled.

Within the first two messages, she knew what she had found. And although she knew there was only venom ahead, she kept reading anyway. It was a simple back-and-forth between Martin and, Danielle assumed, a very needy and exploitive woman. The woman started the conversation.

Her: When you coming back by? It's been 3 days. Can't wait much longer. A girl has needs, you know...
Him: Oh I know. And I plan to meet them. Tomorrow, ok?
Her: You promise?
Him: Yes.
Her: Good. I'm already wet just thinking about it. You can't even imagine the things I'm going to do to you...
Him: Oh, I can imagine plenty. Feel free to send me your ideas and suggestions.

And boy, did she. Danielle would have blushed at some of what she was reading if she hadn't been so irate. *At least now I know why he's always so hesitant to be physical with me,* she thought. *It's because he's got some other woman's smell on him.*

Behind her, she heard the click of the pump. With shaking hands, she closed out of the message thread, pushed the button to put the phone to sleep, and placed it back in the console. She did it all with plenty of time to spare, as Martin didn't open the door for another five seconds.

She wanted to tell him right then and there. To tell him she knew about the other woman and about all of the very descriptive things she wanted to do to him—had probably already done to him, in fact.

But she stayed quiet. She wanted to see just how far he might take it. Maybe the ridiculous fight at the block party was going to uncover some part of him she had not seen yet.

She turned her head away from him as he pulled the car out of the gas station parking lot. As he started down the road, Danielle began to think long and hard about some things. Slowly, a smile crept to her lips and she wasn't even aware of it.

If Chloe had seen it, however, she would have recognized it right away.

But Chloe wouldn't have known what it meant...why the smile was there.

Think you're getting one over on me, do you? she thought, still refusing to look at him. *Let's just see how that works out for you.*

55

And then her mind wandered. It veered and stretched and eventually reached into a place she had not allowed herself to visit in a very long time.

A dark place.

A place she always thought she had left behind but which was always waiting there for her whenever there seemed to be no place else to go.

CHAPTER ELEVEN

As hard as she tried, Chloe could not get the image of Danielle's sinister little smile out of her mind. Something about it gnawed at her, an itch she could not scratch. She wrestled with it on Sunday and it occupied her mind while she and Steven sat around the house, avoiding one another. She could tell Steven was starting to feel ashamed of his actions at the block party but was not quite ready to own his part of it.

Still stumped by why Danielle's nearly passive smile continued to bother her, Chloe started to become aware that there was something there—something that smile seemed to be dragging up from the past. That's why Chloe wasted no time on Monday morning; she called Dr. Skinner's office as soon as she could. She was able to schedule an appointment for one o'clock that afternoon.

As the hour approached, Chloe started to wonder if she had somehow been lying to herself about her past—particularly about what had happened with her mother. She *had* been young and even the shrinks she had seen as a young girl had indicated that such a trauma might never truly be peeled all the way back. It was an idea that was heavy on her heart as she finally stepped into Skinner's office that afternoon.

"You told my receptionist that you had an eventful weekend," Skinner said. "Care to tell me about it?"

She did, with great embarrassment. But getting it out and speaking to someone other than Steven about it was quite helpful. She ended the summary with seeing the devious smile on Danielle's face and how it had seemed to trigger something within her.

"Do you think she simply enjoyed seeing Steven being confronted in front of your new neighbors?" Skinner suggested.

"I honestly don't know," she said. "But the more I thought about it over the weekend, the more I started to think about the day my mother died—about the very scene I walked you through last week. I was wondering if there might be something more there, some memory that might still be muddy."

"And you were hoping I could help to clear it up…if, that is, there is anything at all to be cleared up at all?"

"Yes, that's my hope."

57

"Well, we can certainly give it a try if you are willing," Skinner said. "The last time we attempted it, you seemed very flustered near the end. It's one of the reasons I stopped the session when I did. Are you sure you'd like to try it again?"

She almost said no. She felt like she was expecting some magic trick, for Skinner to reach inside of her head and pluck out the very thing she was looking for. It made her feel naïve and helpless. But before she could utter an answer either way, Skinner seemed to have made the decision for her.

"As you recall," he said, "I need you to make sure you are absolutely comfortable where you are sitting. And that means doing your best to rid your mind of any expectations…of any hopes or doubts. Can you do that?"

She pressed in against the chair, closed her eyes, and was reminded of just how comfortable it was. She also knew that he was going to ask her to concentrate on her breathing, to make sure that every part of her body was relaxed. She did all of that, hearing his voice but not paying much attention to it. She was trying to wipe her mind clear, to forget about the fight at the block party, about Danielle's smile…

"Do you remember the shoes?" Skinner asked. "The Chuck Taylors?"

"Yes."

"Can you still see those laces? The big looping ones?"

She could. And they were exceptionally clear. She could even see the dirt and grime on them.

"Are you back out there on the stoop to the apartment building?" Skinner asked.

She nodded. She was finding it hard to speak. She was intently focused on her shoelaces. Even before Skinner asked her to do so, she stood up, watching the loops on the tied laces shift. "I'm going back inside," she said.

"Good, good. Now this time, though, I need you to try to look beyond your mother's body and the blood. I know it will be hard, but I need you to try. Instead, I want you to give all of your attention to Danielle. Do you think you can do that for me?"

She nodded, understanding that she found speaking difficult because going back to that moment in time had happened incredibly fast this time. She felt dizzy, only in no way she had ever experienced before.

She watched her shoes move up the stairs, into the building, and then to their apartment. She heard her father inside,

58

screaming—he was on the phone, she knew, speaking to someone with 911. But she ignored it as well as she could. As Skinner had asked, she even looked past the shape of her mother's body on the floor. Nope…just the shoelaces, tied loosely and matted with dirt in places.

And then there was Danielle.

"Okay, I'm here," she told Skinner in a sleepy voice. "I see Danielle. She's standing over Mom's body."

"Do you see her as she was that day?" Skinner asked.

"Yes."

Blood on her clothes. A vacant look in her eyes as she stared down at their mother. Yes, this was a ten-year-old version of Danielle for sure.

"Okay, so now I want you to look away from those shoelaces and focus on her. Don't concentrate too hard. Just look at her and wait for it. See if something comes to you."

"It's…no, it's not here. Not *now*. It's something later…after the cops came. We were in the back of our grandmother's car."

"Can you see that car?" Skinner asked. "Can you see your sister in that c—"

The scene switched right away. She was no longer standing at the foot of the stairs by the motionless shape of her mother. She was sitting in the back seat of her grandmother's car. She and Danielle were huddled together. It was the first time Danielle had showed any real emotion. She was crying, but just barely.

Oh my God, I forgot about this, Chloe thought. *How did I….*

"It wasn't him," Danielle said. "It wasn't Daddy. He didn't do this. I know it wasn't him."

From the front seat, their grandmother let out a little moan of sadness.

And it was that noise from the past that seemed to pull Chloe straight out of the memory. She opened her eyes and let out a short, jerky breath. She looked around the office, her eyes finally settling on Dr. Skinner.

"You okay?" Skinner asked.

"Yeah. I…I don't know how I forgot about that."

"Was it the answer you were looking for?"

She thought of Danielle's face in the back of their grandmother's car. There had been genuine sorrow there, real tears and a legitimate expression of grief. While it wasn't what she had been expecting, it seemed to open a few doors that had been closed for quite a while.

"I don't know," she answered honestly.

"Well, while we're here, why don't you tell me how your internship is going?" Skinner asked.

At first, she did it only because he'd asked—purely out of obligation and nothing more. But after a minute or so, she found that the distraction was a welcome one. She'd been so preoccupied with Steven and Danielle that she'd nearly forgotten the true center of her life—interning to become a field agent.

She spent the next half hour talking about the internship as well as what she planned to accomplish over the course of her career. And while it did indeed feel great to start looking into her future and seeing how it was coming into shape, she was also fully aware that it was her past that had helped to form the woman she was right now.

***

She got a text as she was walking out to her car. She checked it, assuming it would be Agent Greene, but did not recognize the number that popped up on her display. The message itself, though, clued her in.

Hey, it's Kathleen. Sorry I didn't get a chance to see you Saturday. Heard about what happened. Sorry to hear it. Hope all is well. Anywho…I'm going out with some ladies from the neighborhood tonight for drinks. Ruthanne Carwile will be there, too. We'd love for you to come. Want you to see that one unfortunate event does not blacklist you! LOL.

At first, Chloe was a bit insulted by it. But she also knew just how easy it was to misread tone and voice in a text message. Based on what she had seen from Kathleen—the overenthusiasm and cheer—she didn't think her old high school friend would invite her out just to belittle her.

And besides, she sure could use a drink.

She thought of the way the crowd had gathered around Steven and Martin as they had fought. She easily recalled the expressions—some laughing, some hiding their heads as if they were too good to witness such a thing. And then, of course, there had been Danielle, detached and smiling.

Yes, she could use a drink. Hell…she could use a *few*.

CHAPTER TWELVE

Danielle spent that night at work, going through her routines and doing her best to push Martin out of her mind. She mixed drinks, poured beers, flirted, even pretended to accidentally get a little water on her shirt from the seltzer hose to get a few great tips near the end of the night.

She had only ever taken two men home from her job at the restaurant bar. The ones who wanted her were easy to spot. They actually *weren't* the chatty ones trying to impress her. They tended to be the quiet ones, sitting at the edge of the bar watching her work. When she spoke to them, they'd respond confidently and make intense eye contact. As vain as it might seem, it was a nice feeling.

As she rounded out her shift that night, there were two of them. She could have had either of them. She knew that and tucked the idea away, taking it with her. Maybe after she was done with this whole Martin thing she'd allow herself another fling. She kept thinking about the texts, the pictures…and what she planned to do in response to them.

When she called last call, she nearly started flirting hard with one of them but decided not to. Too much trouble. Too much drama.

Still, driving home knowing that someone would want her— even if it was a partially drunk man who had been wearing a wedding band—made her feel good. It made her feel valued and wanted. She wondered if Martin thought he was the best thing out there for her…that her options were limited.

Little does he know, she thought as she parked her car in the lot in front of her building. Still on a high from the attention of the bar's patrons, she thought she might take a nice hot shower. She thought she might—

And then it came crashing down when she opened the door and entered her apartment.

There was another note on the floor.

She picked it up and read it. By the time she read it for the second time, her hands were sweating. She slowly walked into the kitchen, rereading it over and over again. It was a cryptic message but she was pretty sure she knew what it meant.

She set it on the kitchen table and read it yet again.

KILL HIM OR I WILL.

She crept over to her window and looked out over the rear parking lot of her building. She wasn't sure what she was looking for. Maybe someone lounging by their car, simply looking like they didn't belong. She wasn't sure. But all she saw was a darkened parking lot, partially aglow in yellow street lamps.

How long ago did they drop this letter off? she wondered. *Did I pass them in the hallway when I came inside the building? Did they drive behind me? Were they at the bar?*

Paranoia sank into her like a knife into her heart. She went to the kitchen counter and grabbed her meds. She popped the top off and looked inside the bottle.

No, she thought. *No. They make the paranoia worse. Ever since Chloe came by and demanded that you get back on them it's been worse, hasn't it?*

She was pretty sure it had been. She put the cap back on and slid the bottle into her junk drawer. She walked back to the note and picked it up, somehow feeling safer when it was in her hands.

KILL HIM OR I WILL.

It was the first letter that had given her an instruction—an order to be followed. And she knew what it meant. But did the letter writer actually *mean* it?

Suddenly, she couldn't stand to be in her apartment. She had to get out of there, had to make sure she was on the move and not staying stationary for the letter writer to come back and wait on her. She grabbed her keys and hurried outside. She did not feel safe again until she was in her car and the doors were locked. And even then she kept glancing into the back seat just in case.

She didn't know where she was going. She thought for a moment that she might drive to Lavender Hills. It was so late…surely Chloe would be home. But no. Then she'd have to tell Chloe about the letters. And God only knew how Steven would react to her dropping by at such a late hour.

She kept checking her rearview. Maybe the letter writer was tailing her, making sure he knew where she was at all times.

KILL HIM OR I WILL.

Martin…that was the *him.* She assumed this, anyway. It just seemed to fit. It felt right. Somehow the letter writer knew him. And maybe the letter writer even knew about the little skirmish at

Chloe's block party somehow. Hell, maybe they even knew about Martin's other girlfriend.

As she thought this, the pictures and messages the bitch had sent went tearing through her head. She fumed, nearly gritting her teeth.

She'd tell him soon. Probably the next time she saw him. If he thought he could mess around on her like that and get away with it, he had another think coming. If he thought Steven had handed his ass to him, he wasn't going to be ready for the hell she would unleash on him.

KILL HIM OR I WILL.

Not a bad idea, she thought with a twinge of morbid humor.

But still, she continued to check her rearview, sure that someone was tailing her, watching her every move.

But she knew that was bullshit. There was no one on her tail. She was in the clear. She was free.

Free, she thought, as her mind wandered back to those messages on Martin's phone. *God, he had me. What a fucking idiot I am...*

A flash of anger raced through her as something new came to her...an idea that was dangerous but seemed to have some merit to it. He'd known she was falling for him. She had not said it in words but she knew he had sensed it. And he had rewarded it by giving her a key to his apartment. She thought about that, about being able to enter his apartment.

And then she had another thought.

His car. It was an old clunker, a Chevy Cavalier that he'd somehow managed to keep running for ten years. It was a piece of shit, but man he loved that car.

With a smile on her face, she thought of where he kept the key—like an idiot, right under the passenger floor mat since the door locks were busted anyway.

Danielle turned around in the nearest parking lot she could find and headed in a different direction. With a devious plan in her mind, she headed for Martin's apartment.

***

Danielle was not running the headlights, so it was hard to see what was coming at her from down the gravel road ahead of her. Gravel pinged up against the bottom of the car in a series of dings. It sounded bad.

Not that she cared. She was behind the wheel of Martin's car now.

She knew this road well, as she had lost her virginity at the end of it at the age of fourteen. She'd come down here with many guys because it was so tucked away and isolated, an old cutaway road for state vehicles back when the water tower at the end of this road still serviced the town of Pinecrest.

But that tower had been condemned in the early nineties and the road was no longer used for anything other than promiscuous teens and defiant hunters when winter came. The road was bordered with pines and maples, blocking out most of the sky.

In the passenger seat, her cell phone rang...again. She ignored it when she saw Chloe's name on the display. It was the third time she'd called tonight.

She came to the end, to the edge of a lake. The lake, she knew, extended farther out into the surrounding woods. It eventually became a magnet for real estate as it filled in the expansive land behind one of Pinecrest's most notable snobby communities—snobbier, even, than Lavender Hills.

She made a U-turn and backed the car up to the edge of the water until she could feel the back tires sinking in the mud. She stopped, put the car into neutral, and waited to see how easily the back end would sink. She was surprised at just how quickly the drop off of the edge of the lake was taking the car, and she feared she might not make it out in time.

She quickly opened the door and scrambled out of the car. When she hit the ground and managed to get up running, she turned and saw that the car was already half submerged in the water.

There was a moment when she feared the front end would get caught in the roughage along the bank, but the weight of the back and the tug of the water freed it. She watched it sink, amazed at how fast it happened.

She did not stick around to reflect on what she had done. It was already eight thirty at night and she had at least a mile and a half to walk back to the main road. From there, she figured there was another mile or two before she would come to the first gas station— the first actual business that a cab would bother to come out and pick her up.

Back in her younger days, she'd simply hitchhike. She'd done it several times and had paid some men for those rides in ways she'd prefer to forget.

That's in the past, she thought as she made her way into the thickness of trees to hide herself away from anyone who might venture down the old state gravel road. *That's not who you are anymore.*

Of course, the question remained…*Who am I, then?*

She tried very hard not to think of the car she had just backed into the lake and how it might be a start to answering that question.

CHAPTER THIRTEEN

The one good thing about having an antisocial and moody sister was that it was usually a given that she would be home so long as she was not at the restaurant working. Chloe relied on this assumption as she approached Danielle's front door at six o'clock that afternoon. She knocked and waited in silence for several seconds. Just as she was about to knock again, she heard the slightest movement on the other side of the door.

"Who's there?" Danielle asked from the other side.

"It's Chloe."

She listened to the sound of the lock being unbolted from the inside and then the door opened quickly. Danielle ushered her inside and Chloe took note of how quickly she closed the door behind them. She almost commented on it but did not want to draw attention to the behavior; better to keep a check on it while she was here rather than give her the opportunity to deny it.

"What are you doing here?" Danielle asked.

"Steven and I have been at odds ever since the block party," she said. "We decided it might be best to take some time apart. Just a day or so."

"This isn't breakup territory, is it?" Danielle asked. "Although...no big loss. You can do much better."

"No, not breakup territory. And God, Danielle...I'm marrying him. You know that, right?"

Danielle shrugged, as if she was already bored with the conversation. "All the same," she said, "I'd hate to think you guys would end it over something my stupid boyfriend did."

"How are you guys?" Chloe asked.

"Same as you and Steven. Not talking. I'll probably break up with him. The more I get to know him, the more of an ass I see he is."

"I'm pretty sure that's the case with all men."

They sat down on the couch and Chloe could already feel an uncomfortable silence settling down around them.

"You had dinner yet?" Chloe asked.

"Yeah. Chinese. Orange chicken. There are some leftovers if you'd like some."

Chloe had actually had a quick dinner already but did not want to miss the opportunity to take Danielle up on free food. Something as simple and kind as offering leftovers was a big step for Danielle. It was frustrating because with every little baby step toward normalcy, there was something like her quickly shutting the door behind them to counterbalance it.

Or that creepy smile from the block party.

"Yes, please," she said.

Danielle walked into the kitchen, got the leftovers out of the fridge, and placed them in the microwave. Chloe watched her sister and almost felt bad for visiting. She had wanted to check in on Danielle, sure. But she was really there to see if she could see any further signs that might resemble that smile—or the vacant and ghostly look she had uncovered from her memories in Skinner's office.

"Danielle…are you okay?"

"Yeah. Why do you ask?" she said from the kitchen.

"You seem…antsy. When I came in, you couldn't close the door fast enough. Is it Martin? Are you worried he'll come by and start trouble?"

"No. He's an ass, but he's not stupid."

"Is it the medicine? Is it messing with your emotional state?"

"I wouldn't know," Danielle said. "I haven't taken it since you were here before."

"Jesus, Danielle. You apparently need it. If it was prescribed to you for mood swings, you need to take it. It's probably why you've been so…"

"So what, Chloe?"

The microwaved dinged. Danielle took the orange chicken out and brought it to the living room. She practically tossed it down on the coffee table in front of Chloe.

Chloe thought of that sinister smile from the block party. Of how she had been so chatty and happy one moment and then pulled into some dark corner of her mind a moment later.

"So all over the place," Chloe safely finished.

Danielle shrugged. She took a seat on the opposite side of the couch and looked toward the door. It was a very quick glance, but Chloe picked up on it. She was also fidgeting, nervously plucking at the fabric of her shirt and finding it hard to sit still.

"Danielle…if something was wrong, you'd tell me, right?"

"Probably not."

"I'm serious."

Danielle sighed and rolled her eyes. "I wish I could explain it to you. I really do. I'm just…I get paranoid sometimes. And maybe it's because I'm not taking the medicine. I don't know. I just…I'm always on the verge of feeling like something really bad is going to happen, you know? And it's been like that forever."

Even as she spoke, she looked toward the door. Maybe expecting someone she did not like to come knocking—maybe expecting an intruder. It was so hard to read Danielle when she was like this.

Chloe nodded. She *did* know. She'd been the same way up until she really started to devote her time and effort to therapy around the age of fifteen or so. She knew for a fact that Danielle had always just dialed it in. And the moment she could make her own decisions, she had stopped going to therapy altogether.

But now something was obviously bothering her. She looked to be on the verge of a panic attack, and Chloe found herself very worried for her.

"Maybe you need to go back to therapy," Chloe suggested. "There's all sorts of unresolved stuff going on, it sounds like. About Mom and Dad."

"Therapy? Yeah, no thanks."

"Then at least take the medicine," Chloe pleaded. "Don't be so stubborn."

Danielle nodded. "I will. I think I have to. I can't keep living this way."

"Do you think you're just very upset about what happened at the block party?" Chloe asked.

"Partly. But…it's beyond Martin. It's just…I don't know. I think I was hoping life would be better than this. Not needing meds to not be a paranoid bitch, you know?"

It broke Chloe's heart to hear her sister letting out these kinds of thoughts. With an awkward smile, she scooted over and put her arm out.

"What are you doing?" Danielle said.

"It's called a hug."

"Oh no."

But Danielle leaned into it and they snuggled together on the couch as if they were seven or eight years old again, back before their mother had been killed and life had beaten them over the head with misfortune. It was in that moment that Chloe realized that although life had driven a wedge between them, that gap was slowly closing. And if there was indeed something wrong with

68

Danielle, be it mentally or emotionally, she was going to be right there by her side until the end.

***

Chloe stayed at Danielle's apartment until Danielle took one of the pills in front of her. They then remained on the couch, saying nothing at all, as they watched the first half of *Pretty Woman*—not because either of them particularity liked the movie but because it was a movie they had grown up on and, as odd as it seemed, was nostalgic for both of them.

An hour later, while Chloe was driving out to meet Kathleen and some of the other Lavender Hills women for drinks, the simple act of having watched that movie tonight helped Chloe to realize something.

She and Danielle were twenty-seven. Danielle was living in an apartment that, while not rundown, was far from luxurious. She also drove the same car she had driven when she had left home at seventeen. Meanwhile, she had roughly two hundred DVDs, God only knew how many CDs, and an overabundance of band T-shirts. It wasn't just that she was still blowing money on music and movies—it was that it was in the form of CDs and DVDs...physical components. While everything else had gone digital, Danielle had remained behind, still preferring to buy the physical items. Chloe had no idea why this struck her as sad but it did. Perhaps it was a characteristic of someone who was unwilling to move on. And if that was indeed the case with Danielle, surely the older familiar entertainment methods were not where inability to move on stopped.

Perhaps it reached all the way back to losing their mother and watching their father get carted off by the police.

It wasn't Daddy. He didn't do this.

She heard that ghost of a memory, spoken in her sister's voice, as she drove out to meet a group of women who could very well turn out to be her central group of friends. How that could still be possible after what had happened at the block party was beyond her, but she wasn't going to start questioning their motives just yet.

They'll never be my friends, though, Chloe thought as she neared her destination. *The looks on some of their faces at the party even before the fight...these people have already made up their minds about me. They probably only want to hang out with me just to get some juicy details about my past.*

69

She thought of Ruthanne Carwile and Tammy Wyler. She thought about how they had been a little too enthusiastic to meet her. And then, of course, there was the suspicious anxiousness she had seen in Ruthanne's eyes.

Maybe I'll dig that out of her tonight, Chloe thought.

But at the same time, this also made her feel left out. Even if she didn't want to admit it, she *wanted* to be friends with these women. And she was afraid that they had already pre-judged her—a fear that hurt more than she had expected.

They met at a little dive bar that Chloe had heard about while in high school but had never actually gotten the chance to visit. Once she was inside, she was rather surprised. It was more like a cocktail lounge than a small-town bar. When she entered, she found Kathleen and two other women sitting in a corner booth near the back, one of whom looked vaguely familiar.

"Glad you could make it," Kathleen said, scooting over in the booth.

Chloe sat down beside her and realized that the other face within the trio looked familiar. "Courtney Braxton?" she asked with a smile.

"The one and only," Courtney said, also with a smile. She had been one of the more popular girls in high school, graduating a few years ahead of Chloe. Her parents had been well-to-do but from what Chloe remembered, it was her willingness to do things with the boys behind the dugouts during PE that had truly made her so popular.

"And then this," Kathleen said, gesturing to the other woman, "as you know, is Jenny Foster. She's been back in Pinecrest for about ten years. She's a fifth-grade teacher at Pinecrest Elementary."

A friendly round of introductions filled the table as a waitress came by with refills and took Chloe's order. She ordered a mojito and did her best to fall into the rhythm of conversation. She quickly discovered that Courtney had been married for four years and that she and her husband had been trying to get pregnant for the last few months. She also discovered a lot of gossip about the neighborhood, none of which she paid much attention to.

"So I have to ask," Courtney said. "I heard about the scuffle between your husband and some other guy. Was it Danielle's boyfriend?"

"It was," Chloe said. "But we're honestly just all trying to look past that now."

"Sure, sure," Courtney said. "Is she okay? Your sister, I mean?"

"Yeah, she doesn't really let things like that affect her very much."

Kathleen chuckled, nodding her agreement. "I remember that about her from school. She just didn't give a damn what anyone thought about her."

"I don't remember her very well," Courtney said. "I remember the two of you looking identical but didn't she change her hair color like every month? And she always wore black, right?"

"Yeah, that was her," Chloe said, doing her best to inflect a tone that indicated she had no interest in discussing her sister.

"Well, I hope she dumps this guy," Kathleen said. "From what I hear, he was drunk or high or something."

"No, I don't think he was," Chloe said. "He and Steven just had a thing. They butted heads right away."

"Steven seems nice," Jenny said. "I met him for a bit just before it all happened."

"Yeah, looks like you got a good one," Kathleen said.

"So how about Danielle?" Courtney asked. "What is she up to these days?"

"She works as a bartender. Keeps a low profile, doesn't really get out much. She seems to like what she does, though."

She was simply speculating there. She honestly had no idea if Danielle liked what she did or not. She just wanted to move the conversation elsewhere without coming off as a bitch.

"Were either of your folks like that?" Jenny asked. It was an innocent question but still rubbed Chloe the wrong way.

"Yeah, a bit," she said. Although, honestly, her father *had* been very much a loner. He had been a friendly and fun man from what she remembered, but had never been very social.

"Maybe that's where Danielle gets it from," Courtney said.

The waitress brought Chloe her mojito, which Chloe started drinking right away to keep a confrontational comment from coming out of her mouth. Apparently, though, what she had planned to say was evident on her face.

"Forgive me for saying so," Kathleen said, "but I never understood her. She was always so pretty—you both were—but back in high school, she never really wanted much to do with anyone. Did she even ever go out and hang with friends or anything?"

"No," Chloe said, now no longer caring what sort of tone came out of her mouth.

"Is she still listening to that dark, angry music?" Courtney asked with a grin.

"I don't know. Are you still giving out hand jobs to any guy that gives you the time of day?"

At once, the trio of friends all looked simultaneously wounded. Apparently, they had not been expecting any sort of kick back. Honestly, Chloe had not either. But *damn,* it felt good.

"I'm sorry," Chloe said, not meaning it at all. "But did you guys want to talk about what's going on in your lives or did you just plan on attacking my sister?"

"Oh, Chloe, we weren't—" Kathleen started.

Chloe's phone buzzed in her pocket. She completely ignored whatever it was that Kathleen was saying to check it. She screamed a bit inside when she saw that it was Sally, her soon-to-be mother-in-law. Still, it gave her an excuse.

"Sorry, have to take this," she said. She took a large gulp of her drink and then walked out to the front of the bar, into a small waiting area.

She read the message, trying to remember a moment in the past year or so of her personal life where she had felt more frustrated. Gossipy neighbors and an overstepping future mother-in-law—it felt like far too much to bear all at once.

The text that had come through read: **What's the status of the wedding invitations? You guys agree on one yet? Clock is ticking if you want to get them out on time. Want to give your guests as much time to plan as possible.**

Why the woman insisted on texting her with these issues rather than Steven was beyond her. Probably because she didn't want to pester her precious little boy. She quickly fired off a text just so Sally wouldn't keep endlessly texting her.

Yup. Final decision in a few days.

She then pocketed her phone, dug a ten-dollar bill out of her purse, and stormed back to the table. She downed the rest of her drink as the other three women watched her. Chloe set her glass down, tossed the ten on the table, and gave a quick little wave.

"Sorry," she said. "Wedding stuff. But this was…well, not fun. But it was *something.*"

Without letting Kathleen, Courtney, or Jenny say another word, Chloe turned and walked back out. It felt good to be a little cruel to women who apparently had nothing better to do than stick their noses in other people's business. Apparently, some things sincerely did not change from high school.

And once more, she was reminded of why she had been so happy to move away from this town when she graduated from high school. And yet her past still dug its claws in…if not in haunting memories of her parents, then in the way people spoke of her family as if they were haunted.

It was just another way her past kept pulling back like an angry and relentless tide. She could only wonder how long she'd be able to fight it here in Pinecrest before she drowned.

CHAPTER FOURTEEN

The next morning, she met Agent Greene at HQ. He was on his phone sending a text when she crossed his path in the lobby. He looked up and smiled, instantly pocketing the phone.

"I was just texting you," he said. "We've got another crime scene to check out. You good taking a partial lead on it?"

"Yes," she said, handing him the coffee. "The other morning was just a fluke. You have my word on that."

"Did you take my recommendation to see Skinner?"

"I did. It was extremely helpful."

"Good. Now, why don't you drive this morning?"

It was a small gesture but meant quite a lot to Chloe. It was a show of trust—a way for Greene to show her that he wasn't afraid of letting her be in control for a while.

They drive out to a small suburban area ten minutes outside of Baltimore. The scene was located in a trailer park where the mobile homes were tightly packed in. As she pulled in behind several local police cars, she saw that many of the residents were swarming the small dirt thoroughfare that wound through the park.

Greene had told her only the basics on the way over, not wanting to affect her judgment too much. All she knew about the scene when she got out of the car was that they were walking into a drug deal gone bad. The FBI was involved because one of the men who had taken part in the deal was a highly wanted suspect in the Philly area for several counts of distributing.

As she and Greene walked up the shaky porch steps—made primarily of what looked like ancient wood and nails—the cops already on the scene seemed relieved. Chloe and Greene showed their IDs and were allowed inside.

Chloe noticed the smell right away. Blood. Garbage. The sticky sweet smell of marijuana—and here it was, just eight o'clock in the morning.

The scene was easy enough to piece together. Chloe stood a few feet inside the door, allowing Greene in as well. They both studied the place closely even though the crux of the story was plain to see directly in front of them.

A couch sat against the far wall of what served as the living room. There were two bodies on it, one of which was slumped nearly off of the couch. This body was missing the top left portion of its head. Blood had been splattered on the walls and was even now still spilling from the grisly wound onto the carpet.

The body beside it was just as dead, a large hole in the lower chest and upper abdomen area. It was gruesome, but she had properly prepared herself. While it was ghastly to see, it was not nearly as bad as what she had envisioned in her mind.

Still...there was a lot of blood. And it was very recent.

Shotgun, Chloe thought. *Close range. My God...*

The person with the wound to the chest had been holding a Glock. It lay discarded and useless by his feet. The Glock, it seemed, had been used to ward off the body that was currently lying in the center of the living room floor. The body was face down, the head turned to the side. From what Chloe could see, he had been shot high in the chest, just under the jaw, and directly under the right eye. Each shot had an exit wound, clearly visible from the back.

"I'll be damned," Greene said. He hunched down to the victim in the floor. He winced at the sight and then shrugged. "This is the guy on our list. Oscar Estevez. The feds have been after him for about three months."

A cop poked his head in the door behind them. "You might want to check the rear bedroom in the back," he said. "We've catalogued it but I'm sure you bureau guys might find it interesting.

Greene nodded and beckoned Chloe to follow him. She did, and they wound their way down the thin hallway to the back of the mobile home. The entire place smelled of mildew and pot; it was so strong near the back of the trailer that it forced Chloe to start breathing through her mouth.

They came to a bedroom in the back of the trailer. The walls were adorned with pornographic posters. An old TV sat on top of a battered dresser. But what really attracted their attention was the fact that the mattress on the bed had been overturned, revealing the box springs. The cover from the box spring had been torn open, revealing several bundles of cocaine. It was all wrapped in plastic and taped up with black electrical tape. At first glance, there appeared to be at least twenty bundles.

"So what do you take away from this scene?" Greene asked

"Well, it looks like the criminals more or less did our work for us. Looks like some sort of drug deal gone wrong. Or a customer came in with a complaint and that went badly."

"Yes. At this point we can only speculate. It looks like a case-closed sort of ordeal but we'll still need to run an investigation. The bad news is that we're still going to be responsible for doing the paperwork and report. So let's go ahead and get a proper investigation of the place—maybe ask some of the locals scattered outside for some more details and—"

Greene's cell phone buzzed, cutting him off. He checked it and said, "One second."

He answered the call and stepped out into the hallway. Chloe was able to listen to his end of the conversation while also checking out the bedroom. She checked the drawers of the bureau and found a scattering of clothes, rolling papers, and several porn DVDs. She found no weapons of any kind, nor any proof that there was anything at play here other than a drug deal that had taken a very wrong turn.

Green came back into the room, his phone still in his hand. "So we need to make quick work of this scene," he said. "We've got another case to check in on. This one is right in your neck of the woods, I believe. Pinecrest, right?"

"Yeah. What's the case?"

"Possible missing persons case," he said. "Some guy named Martin Shields. Nothing too big. Probably just going to let the local PD handle it."

"You said Martin Shields?" Chloe asked, really hoping she'd heard wrong.

"Yeah. Why?"

Her thoughts instantly went to Danielle. Did she know yet? Or had she maybe even been the one to make the call?

"Shit. I know him. Well, sort of. My sister is sort of dating him."

"Really?" Greene asked, taken aback.

"Yeah. I don't think it's serious, but still…"

"Small world," Greene said.

"Exactly."

"If it's someone close to you, we can make it a priority over this, I think," Greene said. "And even if the local boys do want it, maybe I can keep you in the loop if you want."

"Yeah, I'd appreciate that," she said. But the wheels were still spinning in her head, as she wondered how Danielle played into all of it. It was also eerie, considering she had just seen Martin at the block party.

"Honestly, if your sister is dating him, maybe you should call her right now," Greene said. "We can start looking into it while still wrapping this mess up."

Chloe nodded and made her way back down the hall. She managed to not look at the gruesome sight in the living room as she stepped back outside. She pulled up Danielle's number and placed the call.

Danielle answered on the third ring with a sleepy-sounding: "Hello?"

"Hey, it's Chloe."

Danielle have an exaggerated sigh. "Yes, I took my medication today. Now, if you don't mind I'd like to get back to sleep."

"Danielle, when was the last time you saw Martin?"

"Um, the afternoon of the block party. He dropped me off, we were pissed at each other and haven't spoken since. Why?"

"I, um...I'm at work and we just got a call. Someone apparently reported him missing. And an adult has to be missing for at least a day before the report is taken seriously."

"Are you kidding me?" Danielle said. "Missing?"

"That's the repot right now. We're going to be looking into it in a bit. I was thinking maybe you knew something."

"Well, I sure as hell didn't make the call."

"Do you know who might have?"

"Well, he was apparently screwing someone while seeing me."

"Any idea who?" Chloe asked.

"I don't know her name, but I've seen her naked. There were pictures on Martin's phone. So wait...you mean this is for real? He's actually *missing*?"

"I'm hoping to find out for you as soon as I can."

"Well, keep me posted," Danielle said and then ended the call.

But as far as Chloe was concerned, there was absolutely nothing in Danielle's voice that expressed much concern.

CHAPTER FIFTEEN

It was a little maddening to be looking at wedding invitations while she could not get in touch with her sister. Chloe was really hoping that Danielle was only refusing to answer her phone because she was saddened by the news concerning Martin. Still, given the way Danielle had been acting, it was hard to assume the most innocent and safe scenario.

But she wanted to be a good wife, wanted to show Steven that she was just as involved with him and their upcoming wedding as she was about Danielle's well-being. Besides, it wasn't like Danielle hadn't behaved like this before, not answering calls and becoming distant. She was also discovering that she rather enjoyed the process of looking through the designs for the invitations. Given the way the last few days had gone, it was nice to be able to actually enjoy sitting down and trying to finish planning out the wedding.

Things were still tense since the fight but they were at least able to exist within the same room without getting angry. They scrolled through several selections on her iPad, looking at mock designs from the printer Steven's parents had recommended. Yet as they worked toward making a decision, Chloe started to realize that Steven was also distracted. He would give nods and *yeahs* or *sounds good*s whenever needed, but that was about it.

"You okay?" she asked.

"Yeah," he said, though he said it as if he were coming up from out of a deep sleep.

"You seem distracted. Everything okay?"

"Yeah," he said. "Just thinking about some things at work. Tomorrow is going to be a crazy day. Sorry...I guess I hadn't fully unplugged myself from work mode."

She swallowed down the comment that tried crawling its way out of her mouth. *You're distracted, huh? Let me tell you what distracted is. It's knowing that your sister's boyfriend has gone missing and now your sister won't answer her phone. That's distracting!*

"Anything you want to talk about?" Chloe asked.

Steven seemed to think about it for a while before shaking his head. "No. I don't want to make this any more miserable."

"Checking out invitations isn't your thing, huh?"

"Apparently not. Is that okay?"

Chloe shrugged. "Hey, I don't mind making this decision for us."

"Ah, and speaking of making decisions…Mom called today and asked if we wanted to come over for dinner again."

Although Chloe would rather have her fingernails plucked out one by one, she didn't want to cause any further tension. "That's fine," she said. "Just let me know when. If I were you, though, I'd wait a few days. You need to give that eye some time to clear up."

Steven reached up and gently touched the swollen and discolored area right below his eye—the result of the one single punch Martin had successfully landed. It looked much better already, but was still very noticeable.

"Have you even told your mother anything about what happened?" Chloe asked.

"No. No sense in embarrassing myself, I suppose. And I didn't want to have to tell her that it was Danielle's boyfriend."

He left it at that, the insinuation hanging in the air—the insinuation that his mother did not care for Danielle at all. Not that it was any secret.

"Speaking of which," Chloe said. "I was involved in a case today…a case about Martin. He's apparently turned up missing."

"Really? Who called it in?"

"Not sure yet," Chloe said.

"What a joke," Steven said. "That kind of guy, though…you know. No real surprise that he flaked off. Missing…probably not. Probably just jetted off to some other city because he's too unstable to stay anywhere long term."

Chloe let the topic die there. It was clear that he had no interest in her work; he was too preoccupied with trying to appease his mother with the wedding plans. More than that, Steven tearing into Martin would only result in him also tearing into Danielle. And she did *not* have the patience for that.

So they lapsed back into silence after that, once again looking at wedding invitations without any real excitement of the wedding to come.

***

Chloe woke up to the sound of her alarm the following morning. She was still tired from the night before, as thoughts and worries about Danielle had plagued her mind. She sat up in bed, Steven still asleep beside her, and checked her phone in the hopes that Danielle had at least texted during the course of the night.

But there was nothing from Danielle. She did have a text from Agent Greene, though. It read, **A woman named Sophie Arbogast reported Martin Shields missing. Looking into her ASAP.**

Good…at least there was a sense of direction to the case already. She wondered if Danielle knew Sophie Arbogast.

She got out of bed, put on her running attire, and headed out right away. She preferred to run before eating or drinking anything, relying on the exercise to fully wake her up and clear her head. She'd only gone running in Lavender Hills once, and that had been at dusk on her first day as a resident.

She was pleased to find the neighborhood in absolute silence as she started her run at 5:45. The sun was just beginning to puncture the horizon, casting everything in an ethereal pre-morning purple. She had run two blocks before she saw another human being—an older lady sitting on her porch with a cup of coffee, reading from her Bible. At the end of that same block, she passed a man walking his dog but he was wearing headphones and didn't even take the time or courtesy to wave at Chloe.

The running app on her phone told her that she had run 1.79 miles when she saw a familiar face running toward her as she rounded the corner toward another street. She saw Tammy Wyler, their eyes locking at once, and Chloe knew there was no way to avoid her. Unless Tammy was one of those people who took their running *very* seriously, she wasn't going to be able to avoid having to stop and talk to her.

Which was fine, she supposed. But after the block party, it was easy to assume what the topic of conversation would be. She also wondered if Kathleen or one of the others had filled her in on their brief meeting over drinks.

As expected, Tammy slowed her pace significantly as the two women approached one another. While Tammy stopped altogether, Chloe continued to run in place, hoping it would clue Tammy in to the fact that she did not want to stop to chat long.

"I figured you for the running type," Tammy said. "No way someone can stay that slim and pretty without putting in the work."

"Thanks," Chloe said.

"I'm glad we've run into one another," Tammy said, unable to keep in a dumb little snicker at her lame wordplay. "You've been on my mind a lot since Saturday."

Oh, I bet I have, Chloe said.

"Everything is okay," Chloe said, still running in place. "It was just a misunderstanding. It's all smoothed over for now."

"How about Danielle?" Tammy asked. "How is she doing?"

It infuriated Chloe that everyone who had once known Danielle assumed they knew everything about her. When Tammy asked the question, she did it with a very sorrowful tone, indicating that poor Danielle likely needed all the help she could get.

"She's fine," Chloe said.

She tried to think of a happy medium—of a way to save face, spare her sister's fragile reputation, and also stay in the good graces of these women. If she planned to live in this neighborhood for the long term, she had to try to repair whatever damage had been done. She hated the social politics of it all but she knew it was a reality she was going to have to face.

"Well, tell her I asked about her, would you? You know…I heard her boyfriend is missing. Is that true?"

The speed at which news traveled sometimes floored Chloe and now was no exception. She tried hiding her surprise, asking: "How did you hear about that?"

"Oh, news travels quickly around a place like this," Tammy answered, as if she had just read Chloe's thoughts.

"I'm finding that out," Chloe said, unable to hide her disdain.

"Well…true or not, would you let Danielle know I'm thinking about her? She's in my prayers."

"Of course," Chloe said, forcing the words out. "Enjoy the rest of your run."

Without any clear signal that the conversation was over, Chloe resumed her run. She did not like that she was already irritated by the seemingly gossip-centered nature of the people in her neighborhood. It would make things very interesting as she advanced further and further into the bureau. Already, it was placing a strain on her personal life.

Chloe did her best to push that resentment aside for the time being. The mere mention of Danielle from Tammy Wyler had Chloe once again thinking about her sister. It wasn't unlike Danielle to not answer calls or texts, but something felt different this time— especially considering Martin's apparent disappearance.

Something's not right, she thought.

She thought of Danielle's meds. She thought about that eerie smile on her face when Martin had bested Steven in a headlock.

Before she knew it, Chloe was cutting her run short, heading back home. She was going to get an early start today. She was going to leave the house a little early and hope to catch Danielle by surprise.

She hated to be sneaky, but something inside of her—be it instinct or just a sister's nurturing tendencies—was really starting to worry about Danielle.

And with that inclination, the quiet of the morning seemed eerie rather than peaceful.

CHAPTER SIXTEEN

Chloe knew that she'd be waking Danielle up. It was 7:35 when she stopped by the Starbucks along the way, making sure she at least had a peace offering for waking her sister up so early. She knocked on her sister's door, chai latte with two shots of espresso in hand, waiting for the wrath that was sure to come.

Much to her surprise, Danielle looked very much awake when she answered the door. She gave Chloe a skeptical look and then allowed her to enter without saying a word. It wasn't until the door was closed behind them and Danielle had plopped down on the couch that she bothered to speak.

"It's early," she said. "Did you really miss me *that* much?"

"A bit," Chloe said.

She sat down, getting the lay of the land before proceeding. Danielle had clearly been awake for a while. Music was playing in the background and her laptop was opened on the coffee table. A cup of coffee sat adjacent to the laptop. The music was coming from the laptop's speaker, some type of industrial metal that sounded like nothing but humming and static through the little laptop speaker.

"Why didn't you answer any of my calls or return any of my texts?" Chloe asked.

"Because I knew why you were calling. And I still don't have any answers for you."

"You've heard *nothing*? Did he maybe say something the day of the block party to make you think he was skipping town?"

"No. Nothing. He dropped me off, said he'd call when things blew over."

"You said you thought he was seeing someone else," Chloe said. "Did you actually read the text conversations?"

"Not all of them, no. I'd seen her boobs enough and read more than enough dirty texts. That's about all it was, anyway. Not going to get anything worthwhile out of that."

"Are you not worried about him?"

"No," Danielle said. "He's a grown man and he had at least two women that he was seeing. It doesn't seem so strange to me that he

83

might just not be around. Maybe the pressure of two women got to be too much for him and he left town. God only knows how many other stupid women he has on the side."

"Well, we did get confirmation that it *was* a woman who made the call. Does the name Sophie Arbogast mean anything to you?"

Danielle shook her head. "No. Not that I know of." She took the chai latte without making sure it was hers and started drinking it, despite the fact that she still had a cup of coffee right in front of her.

"If I'm being honest," Chloe said, "you're probably right. Maybe he realized he overstepped his bounds at the block party. Even though he came out on top, he could still feel jaded about it all. Maybe he's embarrassed to be around you now and maybe the other woman failed him in some way, too. It's not uncommon for men with no real roots or reasons to stay in one place to just uproot and move at the drop of a dime. I just wanted to check in on you to make sure you're okay."

"I'm fine," Danielle said. "It's not like it's the first time a guy has pulled a fast one on me."

"And you aren't just pulling some rugged tough girl bullshit on me?" Chloe asked.

"No. We only went out for a little over a month. I *was* starting to think that he might be too good to be true, though. He was kind and gentle and I had to actually manipulate him into anything physical. And then...well, then the block party happened and the phone texts and I saw what kind of guy he really was."

"And since then...have you been—"

"Yes, I've been taking the meds."

Chloe got up, feeling that she was doing nothing but managing to get Danielle slowly upset. "Okay. I thought I'd just swing by. After the news I dropped on you yesterday, I just got concerned when you weren't answering your phone. Could you please give me a call if you hear from Martin?"

"Yes. But I honestly don't see him calling. I feel like he exposed himself Saturday; I think he never meant for me to see that side of him."

"Take care, Danielle."

She felt the need to say something else but before the words could come to her, she felt her phone vibrating in her pocket. She took it out and saw that it was Greene calling. She turned her back and walked into the kitchen to answer Greene's call.

"Good morning," she said. "I got your text about Sophie Arbogast. Do we need to visit her?"

"Eventually, maybe. For now, we've got something even better. We got a call this morning about someone spotting a car in a lake. I'm at the scene now and we've been able to confirm the plates. The car belonged to a Martin Shields."

"A body?"

"No. Not yet. We're going to get some folks out here to start dragging the lake in the next hour or so. For now, I'd like for you to meet me. How fast can you get to Monument Lake? The car was discovered off of an old state access road to the old water tower."

"Give me half an hour."

"Sounds good," Greene said. "And listen...this really isn't a bureau matter as of right now. The local cops are running it. But I had asked to be pinged about any movement on the Shields case just because of your connection to it. It took some convincing, but I got Director Johnson to allow us to sort of work it from the sides. So just keep that in mind when you get here."

"Will do," she said. "Thanks for the help."

Chloe hung up and slowly placed her phone back into her pocket. She returned to the living room but did not sit back down. She had to deliver this news and then head to the scene. It was the first moment since she'd started her internship where a case was directly overlapping with her personal life.

And she did not care for it.

"Danielle...that was Agent Greene, my interim supervisor. They just found a car...Martin's car. It was pulled from Monument Lake."

A shock of fear trailed across Danielle's face, an expression that then seemed to morph into concern. For a moment, it seemed like her brain could not quite decide on which emotion to hone in on.

"Oh my God. Is he...?"

"We don't know. So far, there's no indication that there was a body inside."

"Like *just* now?" she asked. "They just now found it?"

"Yeah. I have to head out there. Are you...are you going to be okay?"

"I guess. It's just...well, that's a lot to process."

"This doesn't necessarily mean the worst, you know," Chloe said. "There's no body. Just the car."

"Yeah," she said dimly. "Okay..."

"Danielle…are you going to be okay?"

"Yeah. I'm okay. Just…keep me posted."

"I will," Chloe said. "And you make sure you call me if you start to feel overwhelmed with this, okay?"

Danielle only nodded and looked to her computer with a blank expression on her face. Chloe gave her one last glance and she once again got that feeling of something being off—of something being wrong.

Danielle did not look sad or worried.

Danielle looked *terrified*.

Chloe nearly said something about this but knew that Greene would be waiting for her. Besides, she also knew that Danielle would not talk about her emotional state—not until she'd had significant time to process it all.

So on that note, with an unsettled feeling in her heart, Chloe left her scared sister behind.

CHAPTER SEVENTEEN

Chloe recognized the gravel road right away. While she had never ventured down it in her younger years, it had gained something of a mythical status when she'd been in high school. It had more or less been the Lover's Lane of Pinecrest. Now, it seemed the road had gone to ruin, weeds popping up along the center and the gravel almost nonexistent in places.

When she pulled her car in behind a series of police cars and another car she recognized as Greene's, a tow truck had started to pull the car out of the water. Two policemen were clambering out of the muck along the edge of the lake. She saw that they had attached some sort of cord to the tow truck's original haul, making it easier to pull the car from the water.

A small group of people—about ten in all—were huddled along the edge of the water, waiting for the car to be pulled fully out. She spotted Greene and joined him.

"You speak to your sister about this yet?" he asked her.

"Yes. I was with her when you called me. Question, though: if they are just now pulling the car out, how was anyone able to ID the car beforehand?"

"The back end struck an outcropping of rock about ten yards out. The front end was visible through the water, and you could just make out the license plate number. Now, tell me…what can you establish from the fact that the front end was sticking up?"

She answered as the tow truck pulled forward, pulling the car partially onto the ground. Mud and muck scraped against the underside as it hit the bank.

"It tells me that it was backed into the water. And if it was Martin's way of committing suicide, then that makes no sense. Why go through the precaution of doing that? If it was indeed backed into the lake, it means that whoever was driving wanted to make sure they had ample time to get out. That would lead me to suspect foul play."

Greene nodded his agreement. "So now let's see if the car itself has any answers."

Agent Greene was the only agent at the scene, giving him authority over the situation. Still, he allowed the local cops to have a look as they made notes for their own files. Once that was done, Agent Greene waved Chloe on to follow him as he looked the car over. He handed her a pair of latex gloves as they went to work.

"First thing I'm looking for," Greene told her, "is any sign that there was some sort of rigged setup behind the wheel or on the gas pedal. It's not unheard of for people to get really creative with this sort of thing. Maybe whoever was behind the wheel didn't even have to drive the car into the lake manually. But...as it stands, I don't see anything that suggests that."

Chloe, meanwhile, opened the glove compartment. A little cascade of water came spilling out as the flap dropped. She rummaged around inside and found nothing of interest: insurance documents, a pack of gum, a few discarded CDs. A few of the CDs were the exact sort of thing Danielle would listen to. Something about this made Chloe feel very protective of her sister—like she was suddenly too close to the scene for some reason.

"Anything good?" Greene asked.

"Nothing," she said, closing the glove compartment.

They then checked under the seats, looking for anything that might provide clues. It took less than two minutes to discover that there was nothing there.

As they closed the door, Greene looked to the trunk. It made sense to Chloe; she'd assumed they'd end up popping it open anyway. But based on what they had found in the car, she was fully expecting to find nothing more than a spare tire.

Greene looked back over to the huddled group of policemen, still eyeing the car. "Sheriff, you got the equipment to pop this trunk open?"

One of the men nodded and instantly walked over to one of the patrol cars. He rummaged around in the trunk and came back with a tool that Chloe had only seen once before. It looked like a modified screwdriver with a heavier head. She knew that there was no finessing to getting a trunk open so the tools used for the job seemed rather primitive.

The sheriff took his tool to the back of Martin's car and placed it roughly into the lock along the back of the trunk. Another policeman had gone to his car to get a short and stubby-looking pry bar, just in case. But as it turned out, the bar wasn't necessary. There was a clattering noise and then a very audible unlatching sound as the trunk popped open.

The sheriff looked inside for a moment and then directly at Greene.

"Bingo," he said.

Chloe and Greene peered into the trunk. Chloe felt as if she'd been slapped across the face when she spied the body in the trunk. It was unmistakably Martin. He looked up at them with featureless eyes, as if he didn't really care much one way or the other that he was dead. There were two large puncture wounds along his chest, one directly above his heart. They were both very obvious stab wounds.

As she looked down at the body, an alarming thought went through her head.

Has Danielle told anyone else about how she found out that he was cheating on her? If so...shit...she could end up being a suspect. And the meds she's been taking and skipping whenever she feels like it certainly isn't going to help matters.

"Well, at least now we know it certainly wasn't suicide," Greene said. He then looked over to Chloe, biting back a frown. "You going to be too close to this one to take part?"

She almost said yes. The idea that Danielle would likely have to eventually be questioned did not sit well with her. But at the same time, she knew she had to remain professional.

"No, I'm good."

"Okay," he said. "So here's the good news for this situation. The body is fresh and wet. If there were any sort of traces of the killer left on him, they'll be quite easy to pull. Especially hair...like this one..."

He trailed off and leaned closer to the trunk, nearly reaching inside. With a gloved hand, he pointed to a stray hair on Martin's right forearm. It wasn't much longer than the hair on Martin's head.

And while it was wet, it was still pretty clear to see that it was black. And short.

Like Danielle's.

CHAPTER EIGHTEEN

Chloe felt the day blaze by her in the same way time seems to pass ridiculously fast in the moments following a car accident or some other traumatic event. She felt like the day was pushing her hard toward something that was going to crash down on her. She kept thinking of Martin and Steven fighting—and of that sharp little smile on Danielle's face as it had happened.

She had elected not to call Danielle. Not yet. She wanted to have that stray hair analyzed and studied, wanted to make sure all bases were covered before she contacted Danielle. She knew nothing could be done in a concrete manner without getting a DNA sample from Danielle, but she also knew there could soon be enough reason to arrest Danielle and then collect the sample.

Still, as she waited in the lab for the results of the hair and a partial fingerprint that had been discovered on the edge of the trunk, Chloe kept looking at her phone. And while she did, there was one thought that kept bouncing around in her head, a thought she hoped was just the result of an overreaction.

Oh God, Danielle, what did you do? What did you DO?

While she waited, she worked closely with Greene in one of the lab's empty offices as they tried to find anyone who would have seen Martin in the last day or so of his life. They used phone records and the people who were known to have seen him last. Because of the block party, Chloe was forced to offer up her own name, as well as Danielle's.

"I can question her for you if you'd like," he said.

"No, I'm okay with it."

"You sure? It's a hell of a lot to put on an intern."

When she only nodded, Greene looked away. "You know," he added, "if she'll submit to a DNA test, maybe we can rule her out anyway."

"The DNA test off of the hair takes what...eight hours?" she asked.

"If the hair is in good condition and fresh—as this one is—it can be as quick as five hours."

Just as it seemed that Greene was going to offer some words of comfort, a knock sounded at the door. Another intern poked his head in, a guy Chloe had only met a few times who worked closely with another agent in the realm of information gathering.

"Two potential leads for you," he said. "We've got a friend of the woman who placed the missing person's call. Says Martin Shields hit on her all the time. Says they hooked up one time at a party a few months back. She doesn't seem at all surprised that he wound up dead in a lake."

"She available to talk?" Greene asked.

"Yes. She's waiting for a call."

"What's the second lead?" Chloe asked.

"We ran Martin Shields's credit card report. The last thing purchased on it was fifty-one dollars in gas. We checked with the station it was purchased at and they're cueing up the security footage from the parking lot. They think there's a chance we might be able to get a look inside the car."

"Thanks," Green said as the intern handed them his findings and took his leave. Agent Greene then seemed to think very hard about something before getting to his feet and sighing.

"Here's what we're going to do," he said. "I'll go check out this woman who claims to have slept with Martin. No sense in you getting your hands dirty in that social triangle of your sister's life. You check into the gas station."

"What about Danielle?"

"I'll send some of the cops down there in Pinecrest to speak with her."

"Any chance I can talk to her first? This is…this is messed up."

"Sorry, I misspoke earlier; I can't let you do that. Personal ties and all. Surely you understand."

"I do. And surely you understand that I know my sister. She didn't do this…there's no way. Please…give me just a few minutes to let her know what's coming."

Greene thought about it for a moment and then lowered his voice, even though they were alone. "I get it. Family is family. It's a peculiar situation for sure. You talk to her, but know that if she leaves town or skips out on us, it falls on you. I trust you, Chloe. So I'm putting a lot of that trust on you right now. Do the gas station first and then talk to your sister. But if something does come out of it, I need you to contact me with details right away."

"Thank you," she said. "Will you get in any trouble for this?"

"No. Technically it's not *outside* the lines of protocol. Any humane agent would extend the same courtesy to a veteran partner.

So yes…I'm sure. Just, get going *now.* Once these results come in…"

Chloe nodded, certain where he was taking the comment. She grabbed up the information on the gas station and Martin's credit card and headed out of the room. As she made her way to the front of the building, she passed by the door that contained the lab that was currently working with the hair and print found at the lake.

Her heart skipped a beat and she hurried by. And once again, as she headed out to her car, that same thought blazed through her head like a comet.

What did you do, Danielle?

***

The gas station in question was less than three miles from Danielle's apartment. She arrived at 11:25 and there was practically no one there. A few customers milled around inside looking at snacks and magazines but the cashier was very cooperative and happy to help her. He'd already been notified that Chloe would be coming so he had cued up the footage in question.

After getting another employee who had been stocking the shelves to cover the register, the cashier took her to the back of the store. There, a small supply room was tucked away, filled with boxes of snacks and impulse buy items. In the far right corner, there was a small setup for the security system. One large screen showed six different camera angles from out in the parking lot. Another screen showed two angles from within the store, and a third from directly behind the cash register.

"The car the cops were asking me about comes in right here," the cashier said, pointing to the center angle at the bottom of the screen.

After several seconds, Martin's car did indeed creep into view. It parked under the awning of one of the six pumps outside. Once it was under the awning, it was impossible to see who was in the car.

"Can you back the footage up and then slow it down?" she asked.

"Yeah. And I can pause it when you need me to. Just tell me when."

The cashier backed the footage up, causing Martin's car to speedily vanish backward out of the screen. He then played the footage forward, slowing it down significantly. The car came into frame and then, for a moment, nearly filled it.

"Pause it," Chloe said.

The cashier did as he was asked. The car's passenger side was facing the camera. She could easily the see the shape of a person on the inside. But from the distance between the camera and the car, as well as the distortion caused by the passenger side window, it was hard to see any details.

"Can you zoom in a bit?" Chloe asked.

"Yeah. But it'll be grainy."

The cashier typed in a command on a security system that Chloe was beginning to understand was a bit outdated. The footage zoomed in a bit, bringing the figure in the passenger seat into view. The cashier had been right; the footage was incredibly grainy.

But that didn't matter. Because Danielle's likeness was unmistakable. Her head was even partially turned in the direction of the camera, making it much easier to identify her.

Really, it came as no real surprise. After all, Danielle had left the block party with Martin. And according to the timestamp on the security footage, this occurred about half an hour after Martin and Danielle had taken their leave.

Still, this was proof. This was enough evidence for the FBI—aside from herself, of course—to eye her as a potential suspect.

"Thank you," Chloe said, her voice low and trembling.

She backed away from the footage slowly but by the time she was back out in the store, she was practically dashing for the door. She had to get to Danielle and speak to her one on one before the hammer came down on her.

And based on the evidence, she didn't think it was going to take too long.

CHAPTER NINETEEN

Chloe was doing everything she could to not assume that Danielle was guilty or that she had any information pertaining to what had happened to Martin. Yet when she saw that her car was parked in front of her apartment building, she was relieved. That would at least show that she was not trying to evade any conversations about the topic. If she was guilty of anything, the chances would be good that she'd be moving around rather than sitting idly in her apartment.

Chloe knocked rapidly on Danielle's door. "Danielle, it's me. I need to speak to you right away!"

She heard a quick series of footfalls on the other side of the door as Danielle responded. She opened the door and looked almost like a different person. She couldn't quite figure out why at first but then she saw it as clear as day in Danielle's eyes.

She looked scared.

Chloe had seen her paranoid and out of sorts. It had been her state most of the time during the last few times they'd been together. But Chloe wasn't sure that she had ever seen her sister *scared.* And that, in turn, scared Chloe.

"What's wrong?" Danielle asked.

"It's Martin," Chloe said, realizing for the first time the weight of the news she was about to deliver. "His body was found in the trunk of his car. I'm sorry…"

Danielle nodded and bit at her bottom lip as it quivered. "My God. I just…how did this happen?"

Chloe walked in without being formally invited and turned to Danielle. "I'm only going to ask you this once and I'm going to believe your answer no matter what," she said. "Danielle, did you have *anything* to do with what happened to Martin?"

"No," she said, wiping a tear away from her left eye. "Nothing."

Chloe had expected Danielle to seem offended at the insinuation. But she was currently too frightened to be offended, or so it seemed.

"I know this is a shock and you need to process, but we don't have much time."

"Time?" Danielle asked, clearly not understanding.

"Danielle...there was a stray hair and a partial fingerprint discovered at the scene. They're both being analyzed right now. And based on what we know at the moment, you were the last person to see him alive. And the hair...it was black and short, like yours. There's footage of the two of you pulling into a gas station and that's the last recorded evidence of Martin's whereabouts."

"Okay, but what does that mean?" Danielle asked.

"It means that in the eyes of any respectable investigator, it's going to appear as if you had something to do with it. That if you didn't kill him, you at least know something about it. So Danielle...please. I need you to be honest with me. Tell *me* the truth before another agent has to speak with you."

Chloe watched as her sister's face went through several different emotions. For a moment, it looked like she was going to break into a sobbing fit. Then she looked almost angry. After another handful of seconds, she simply sat down on the couch and looked blankly at Chloe.

"He loved that stupid car," she said. "And when I found that he was cheating on me, something snapped. I know it's stupid but...I'm always the one to screw people over, you know? I'm not used to being the one getting fucked over. And then the thing at the block party...I felt like he had tried to fool me just to serve some purpose. So...I got his car and I backed it into the lake. Just to get back at him. Just to be a bitch."

"Jesus, Danielle...how'd you even end up with the car?"

"It's a piece of shit. All busted up. The locks don't work and he showed me a while back where the key was...it was one night when we were out drinking and he got hammered and couldn't drive. So I just waited around a bit...when I knew he'd be asleep. I parked my car a few blocks away and walked to his apartment building to take it. But I had no idea the body was in the trunk. Chloe...I swear it."

"God, Danielle. That was unbelievably stupid. What the hell?"

"I know..." she said, close to tears—a state Chloe had rarely seen her in.

"Danielle, if that's your hair on him...or if there's any evidence of you having driven the car, you're going to be in a lot of trouble. Do you understand that?"

"Yes, I do. But...Chloe, what if there's someone else?"

"What do you mean?"

"I think someone might be trying to frame me for this."

"That's a very strong accusation," Chloe said, already praying that it might somehow be true. "What makes you think that?"

For the second time in the last few days, Chloe could tell there was something on the verge of her tongue, something she wanted to say but could not bring herself to do so.

"Danielle, you have to tell me anything that might clear you of this."

"There's nothing," she said.

"Fine. Then I at least need to know what else happened that day after Martin stopped to put gas in his car."

"Nothing. There really wasn't even a *goodbye* between us."

Chloe sighed, feeling herself being pushed toward panic. She knew there was really nothing she could do for Danielle at this point. But she wondered if she could at least buy her sister some time.

It'll come down to the hair and the print, Chloe thought. *Maybe it'll come back inconclusive or maybe even with this other woman's hair on it...*

"Danielle, I need you to stay here," Chloe said. "Depending on what becomes of the prints and the hair, there's a good chance someone from the bureau will want to talk to you. And if you're not here and are hard to get in touch with, that's going to be a bad sign."

"I'm not going anywhere," she said. "Chloe...I know it was stupid. But I just got so fucking angry at him. I didn't know what to do..."

"Yes, it *was* stupid. And immature and....*fuck!* Danielle, I love you dearly but you need some serious help."

With that, she stormed toward the door. She hated to abandon Danielle in that moment but if she stayed there, she was going to lose her cool and really grill her. She stormed out and went back to her car. She felt tears welling up, tears for her sister and the incredibly awkward situation that would soon arise between them.

She was headed back to HQ, planning to visit the lab again. She made it about three miles into the trip when her phone rang. It was Greene, and from the very first word—a tired-sounding *hello*—she could tell that he did not have good news.

"Hey," he said. "I've got nothing but bad news. First, Sophie Arbogast claims that she hadn't seen Martin for three days. They were supposed to meet up two nights ago. She sent him some provocative messages, and she said they always made him return her texts or calls. I've got some guys looking into her story in terms of alibis and it seems like hers are going to check out."

"Is that all?" Chloe asked.

"No. Where are you right now?"

"Between Danielle's apartment and HQ."

"So you already spoke with her?" he asked.

"Yes." She wanted to go ahead and tell him about how Danielle had driven the car into the lake but could not bring herself to do it.

"Well, you might want to turn back around and go back to her place. They found a salvageable print on the key to Martin's car. A very fresh one. Chloe...I'm so sorry...but it's a match for Danielle."

That's when the tears *did* start coming and they came quickly and with force. Chloe excused herself from the phone and then turned the car around the next chance she got.

She was going to have to go back to Danielle's and somehow face the fact that her twin sister was the prime suspect in what was looking to be a pretty blatant murder.

CHAPTER TWENTY

Chloe watched the whole thing happen and it was like having an out of body experience. She was both surprised and saddened to see that Danielle really didn't even fight it. She didn't protest too much and there were very few arguments. Greene stood with Chloe while another agent put handcuffs on Danielle and started leading her out of the apartment.

Danielle only looked at Chloe once, right in the middle of having her rights read to her. There was a heartbreaking stare between them in that moment—a moment in which Chloe realized just how broken and lost her sister was. It was also a look that made Chloe feel that maybe—just *maybe*—Danielle would have been capable of killing Martin. Even though Danielle had admitted to sinking the car—something that would surely come up in questioning—did that mean she could kill him, too?

Maybe…maybe she *did* do it.

She felt her heart breaking as she looked at her sister. *Maybe if I'd been a better sister over the years…reached out and tried to get to know her better. Maybe then I would have seen this coming…*

It started to sink in, a dark reality that she could feel on her like cobwebs. But still, it just made no sense. For one thing, how the hell would frail little Danielle have lifted the rather built body of Martin enough to get him into the trunk?

These thoughts whirled in Chloe's mind as she walked out behind the other agent who escorted Danielle through the doorway.

"Do you have a lawyer?" Chloe asked.

"No. And don't talk to me. You turned me in, didn't you? You didn't even give me a chance. You thought it was me right away."

"Danielle, I—"

"I said don't talk to me," Danielle snapped.

"I'll see that you get a good one. I'll—"

"Don't," Danielle said. "I don't want you involved in this."

Chloe did as her sister asked. She stopped talking as she walked along with the agent, who led her to a generic black sedan. Chloe watched helplessly as Danielle ducked down and got into the back seat. The agent closed the door and then shot Chloe an apologetic look before getting behind the wheel.

Chloe's thoughts flashed back to the morning she and Danielle had watched her father ushered into the back of a police car. For a moment, it felt like her life had come full circle.

"Will they take her to HQ?" Chloe asked Greene.

"Yeah, at the start. They'll interrogate her there. Depending on how that goes, they might move her. I imagine they'll angle for a DNA test, too. To try to match that stray hair they found on Martin's arm. I doubt they'll keep her long. Really, this doesn't have the weight of a bureau case. Pinecrest PD will likely wrap it up."

"I need to go," Chloe said. "I need to be with her."

"Give it some time," Greene said. "You know how the system works. You can be there right away but you won't get to speak with her for a while. Let the feds to their job. I'll make a call for you. I'll make sure you're allowed to speak with her as early as possible."

Chloe nodded and did her best to keep the tears from coming. She'd already almost puked in front of Agent Greene. Did she really want to *cry* in front of him?

"I want you to go home," Greene said. "Take the rest of the day. I'll cover with your supervisor."

"You'll call me when she's available to talk?"

"Absolutely. Do you need a ride? Are you going to be okay?"

"I don't know," she said.

And with that, she turned her back and headed for her car. The tears came right away now, and she did everything she could to not let Greene see them.

***

It was rare that Chloe allowed Steven to see her in a vulnerable state but that's exactly what he saw when she returned home. He was sitting on the couch, slipping a card into an envelope. She saw that it was a thank-you card for the tailor who had helped him with acquiring the perfect tuxedo for the wedding.

"You're home early," he said, uninterested. But then he saw her face, the clear signs that she had been crying, and got to his feet. "What is it?" he asked.

She told him everything. She told him about Martin's car...about Martin's body being found in the trunk and the stray hair and the fingerprint. She told him where Danielle currently was and how something just didn't seem to fit.

"Are you sure?" Steven asked. "I hate to mention it, but you *did* say that she was skipping some medicine to help with mood swings, right?"

"I did," Chloe said. "But even though I don't really know my sister, I know her well enough to know that she's not capable of killing someone."

Do you, though? she wondered, thinking of the sinister smile from the block party.

They sat down on the couch, Chloe feeling the weight of the day finally pressing down on her. She watched as Steven sealed the thank-you note. It actually made her feel a bit better to see that he was actually taking initiative in *anything* related to the wedding.

"What can I do for you?" Steven asked.

"Nothing," she said. "Just…just be here right now. I don't know how to handle this, Steven. And I just need you to be here for me. No snide comments about Danielle, okay? Can you do that?"

He put an arm around her, drew her close, and kissed her on the side of the mouth. "Of course I can," he said.

And he did. They sat together on the couch like that for a very long time. And while it was comforting, Chloe couldn't help but wonder what she had missed during those years she and Danielle had spent apart. What had Danielle been through? Had she encountered something that had shaped her in some unimaginable way—maybe even some way that would indeed make her capable of murder?

The scary part was that Chloe simply did not know the answer.

Scarier still was the fact that she'd likely find out within the next few days.

***

Chloe skipped her morning run the following day. She simply didn't have it in her. Her stomach was a knot of worry, nearly to the point of making her feel sick. She had a cup of coffee but was unable to eat much breakfast. She kept looking to her phone, waiting for Green to call or text.

He finally did, just after seven o'clock. "You're going to be mad at me," he said.

"Why's that?"

"We were given permission for you to talk to her around midnight. But I wanted you to get a good night's sleep. This isn't looking good for her, which means these next few days could be very long for you."

She *was* angry at first but was then able to see the care in his gesture. He was just trying to look out for her.

"Are you there right now?" Chloe asked.

"No, but I'm on the way."

"Then I'll see you in about half an hour."

She ended the call and took her uneaten breakfast of eggs and sausage links to the kitchen counter. Steven was sitting at the bar, scrolling through his newsfeed on his phone, slowly eating a bowl of oatmeal.

"You want this?" she asked, offering the plate.

"Sure," he said. "Who was on the phone?"

"Agent Greene. I've been cleared to go speak with Danielle."

"Oh," Steven said. "Do you think that's a good idea?"

"Why wouldn't it be?" Chloe asked.

"I don't know," he said. "It's evident that you feel certain she didn't do it. But if you go down there around people you're going to have to eventually work with and most of them think she *did* do it…that could cause some tension."

"You're absolutely right," she said. "But this is my sister. I have to be there for her."

When he nodded and sighed, his frustration was apparent. Chloe thought it might be something they'd need to discuss at some point. But for now, she was more interested in getting to her sister.

As she gathered up her things and headed for the door, Steven called out to her. "If you think you're going to be late getting home today, let me know. Don't forget, we're supposed to go to my folks' house for dinner tonight."

"Yeah," she snapped. Being around his parents was about the last thing she wanted to even think about considering everything that was happening. And the fact that Steven could even mention it right now was maddening.

She left the house without another word and made the drive to Baltimore. It was a tense ride as her mind pinballed back and forth between Danielle's situation and the growing turmoil between her and Steven. Deep down, she supposed this current situation with Danielle would really show Steven's true colors. Would he support her while Danielle went through this hell or would he continue to voice his disdain for her?

It was a selfish way to think, but she knew that in one way or another, her own life would be significantly different when all of this came to an end. She could beat herself up over not being an attentive sister all she liked, but it would change nothing. But if Danielle came out of this unscathed…well, things were going to have to change.

When she parked in the parking garage beside HQ, she did her best not to break into a sprint toward the building. When she entered, there were people looking at her with sympathy, some managing a nod of greeting while others quickly looked away.

As she made her way back to the interrogation rooms, Greene met her with a cup of coffee in hand. He gave it to her with a look of worry in his eyes.

"What's that look?" Chloe asked. "Is there something wrong?"

"No, not really. But we told her that you were coming to speak with her. We figured it might help to lift her spirits, you know? But she's refusing to see you."

"What?"

Greene led her into a nearby vacant conference room and closed the door. "She's in a bad state," he said. "I think she's afraid that she's disappointed you. She'd depressed and honestly just doesn't want to talk to anyone."

It broke Chloe's heart a little to hear these things, but she supposed she understood.

"She thinks I turned her in. She thinks I automatically assumed she's guilty."

"Yes, that too."

"Has she said anything that indicates she killed him?"

"No. But her alibis aren't strong at all. Being antisocial by nature, she doesn't really have much to offer. No one other than Martin would have seen her. She said she saw and spoke to you between the block party and the discovery of the car, but the time scale really doesn't even matter. It couldn't be used as a reliable alibi."

"You have to know…this is impossible for me to believe," Chloe said, almost pleading. "She has her issues, sure…but she's not a killer. At least I didn't think so. But…Jesus, I just don't know now. It doesn't seem like my sister, you know?"

Greene seemed hesitant to say anything. After a moment of thought, though, he finally said: "I think I believe you. But for now, we have to go with what the case gives us. You understand that, right?"

"I do," she said. "Thanks for the support. Look…there's this medicine she's on for her mood swings. I don't know which drug, honestly. Is there any way for you to check in to see if she's taking them?"

"She is," he said. "She requested them not too long after she got here. We had an agent go back to her apartment to get them."

"Good. Thanks."

"I can't imagine how tough this is for you. But keep a level head. I know you have to be a sister first, but this is a great time to prove that you can be an effective agent above all else. I know it might not be where your head is at right now, but this is an opportune time to prove yourself."

"That's a sobering thought," she said with a shaky laugh.

But the more the comment stuck with her, the more she could appreciate it—and the more determined she became to find some way to prove that Danielle was innocent.

CHAPTER TWENTY ONE

After the heartbreak of finding that Danielle was refusing to speak to her, Chloe decided to let it ride out for another day or so. While they had spent a great deal of time apart these last few years, Chloe felt like she knew her sister well. Danielle was going to clam up for a day or two, an adult version of the silent treatment. After that, she might allow some people in—hopefully her.

With an assurance from Greene that she'd still have access to Danielle tomorrow, Chloe headed out for the day. She went home and was once again anxious to see how Steven would react to all of this. She found herself wondering if he'd be supportive or relieved that his troublesome sister-in-law was out of the equation.

She rummaged around the house for an hour or so, trying to keep herself busy by cleaning, anything to keep her mind from obsessively latching onto Danielle. When she heard Steven pull up shortly after four o'clock, she felt like she was on the battle lines of some war no one knew was being waged. They had dinner with his parents tonight, and God only knew that was stressful enough. Adding all of this drama with Danielle was doing nothing more than firing the first shot.

Steven came in and seemed to be in a good mood. He usually was when he found her already home when he arrived home from work.

"Short day?" he asked.

"Yeah."

"Any movement on the thing with Danielle?"

She was a little surprised that he'd asked so blatantly. She was also surprised to find that there appeared to be genuine interest in his voice.

"No," she said. "Nothing yet."

He nodded and made a *hmm* sound of acknowledgment before heading off to the bedroom. Chloe had not realized until after they had been engaged just how tied down to his parents Steven was. Whenever they met with his family for dinner, he always made sure to get there on time. Even when they had visited them before they had moved back to town, even if it was out at a restaurant, Steven got stressed out about being on time. That was why she fully expected him to emerge from the bedroom ten minutes from now changed and completely ready for dinner—even though they weren't due to arrive for another hour and a half.

The fear that his parents might suffocate them a little had come to her before. But now that they were beginning to live out that reality, Chloe could feel it sinking in like a needle into her skin.

***

While Sally Brennan had more than enough of her faults, there was one positive to the woman: she could cook her ass off.

When Chloe sat down to Wayne and Sally Brennan's table that night with their baby boy, she had prepared a rack of lamb, seasoned asparagus, and a from-scratch salad that was accompanied by a homemade vinaigrette. The pleasantness of the food itself didn't last very long, though. Sally didn't seem to be able to go a whole five minutes without throwing out a barrage of questions.

"Steven, what's the bruise on the side of your head?" Sally asked.

Chloe winced a bit. She'd thought the bruising from the fight with Martin had faded enough so that Sally and Wayne wouldn't see it. Now the ball was in Steven's court. Would he gladly tell them that Danielle had brought a guy to their house that had made an ass of himself at a block party and started throwing punches? Or would he—God help us all—lie to his mother to help his soon-to-be-wife save some face?

"Oh my God, it was the stupidest thing," Martin said. "I left the medicine cabinet open the other night. I turned away for a moment and then turned around to walk back into the bedroom and ran right into the damned thing. The bruise was pretty nasty for the first day or two."

Wayne Brennan actually laughed heartily at this. "You always were sort of a klutz," he said, taking a large gulp of his glass of red wine.

"Still am, I guess," Steven said.

He reached under the table and gave her hand a little squeeze. *That was for you,* the gesture seemed to say.

There was silence at the table for a moment, broken only by the clinking of silverware against the plates. An uncomfortable feeling started taking root in Chloe's stomach as she noticed the thin and rather restrained look on Sally's face.

Then she spoke, and Chloe understood the uncharacteristic silence at the Brennan dinner table. She'd been holding back, trying to find the right time to drop her little bomb.

"Forgive me for asking," Sally said, looking directly at Chloe. "But I've heard from two different people that your sister was arrested on some absolutely ghastly chargers. Some are saying murder! That can't be right, can—"

"Mom…" Steven said, not only surprised but looking a little appalled as well.

"Well, I just wanted to know," Sally said, as if she was the one being attacked. "After all, if it's true and Danielle is going to be…preoccupied…it *does* affect the wedding."

"With all due respect," Chloe said, "my sister is being held for something she did not do. I haven't really been thinking too much about the wedding."

"Is there anyone else you can ask to take her place?" Sally asked.

The absolute nerve of this woman, Chloe thought. Sure, they were footing the bill for the vast majority of the wedding, but she was taking that responsibility like some sort of priesthood. To say she was using it as a control over Chloe was not overstating things. But now with this new development with Danielle, she apparently felt she had more leverage.

Fuck that, Chloe thought.

"No, not really," Chloe said. "And if it's bothering you that badly, Mrs. Brennan, maybe we should start talking about postponing the wedding."

The look on her face made it clear that she had not expected such a tactic from Chloe. She looked like someone had slapped her, being so dramatic as to even recoil from the comment.

"Oh, I hardly think so," she said. "I've already reserved the grounds at Elder Gardens! I don't see the need to make so many other people change their plans just because of your sister's misfortune."

"I didn't insinuate that," Chloe said. She had much more on the tip of her tongue but she bit it all back. Instead, she got to her feet and looked over at Steven. "Please…take your time in finishing. Enjoy your dinner with your parents. I'll be waiting in the car when you're ready."

"Chloe," Wayne said, using a rare authoritative tone. While he could be equally as annoying as Sally, he at least pretended to be a rational and kind human being most of the time. "This is a little rude of you."

"I'm so sorry," she said. "Maybe we should think of someone to replace *me* in the wedding, too, huh?"

"Chloe, please," Steven said.

"Oh, please," Sally said. "Are we going to pretend that this is really a surprise? We've always known Danielle was trouble. A rotten little girl from the start from what I hear."

"What you hear?" Chloe asked. "Do you always believe what you hear? Are you capable of thinking for yourself and forming your own opinions?"

Again, Sally's reaction was borderline comical in its drama. And Chloe was well aware that there might be something slightly wrong with her…because she loved seeing that look of faked pain on the woman's face.

But Chloe had heard enough. She walked away from the table, never looking back. She did just as she had said: she walked out to the car, got in the passenger seat, and closed the door. She sat there for a moment, staring at her phone. She wondered if it would do any good to call Greene and see if there was any way she could talk to Danielle. Even if she was refusing to speak to her, Chloe figured there had to be *some* way to get around that.

She went over the facts of the case in her head, mainly to obliterate her hatred for Steven's parents and this gossipy little community. It had been just two days. Two days and the grapevine had spread its sticky tendrils into the ears of Sally Brennan.

It was 7:47 when Steven came out to the car. That meant that he had stayed inside for another fifteen minutes after she walked out. Chloe could only imagine the sorts of vile things they had been saying about Danielle while she had been absent. Hell…they had probably gone so far as to convince Steven to call off the engagement.

He got behind the wheel, cranked the engine to life, and pulled out of the driveway. Three minutes passed before he said a word.

"That was a bit of an overreaction," he said.

"Was it? I think it was incredibly rude—and, might I add, calculated—to say something as stupid as that. She didn't wait for me to confirm or deny what people were saying. All she was worried about was who would fill my sister's slot on her little charts and guides she's making for the wedding. Which, by the way, is *absolutely* going to her head."

"Chloe, that's my mom. Want to watch your tone?"

"My *tone*? Are you even serious right now? She has no right to talk about my sister like that!"

"Chloe…you said it yourself the other day. The case against her is pretty solid. It looks like there's only one outcome. And Mom might be right."

"How so? Say whatever you're going to say, Steven."

"Fine. I don't think it's completely out of line for myself or for my mother to *not* want a murder suspect participating in the wedding."

Her first urge was to punch him. And she had never felt that way toward him before. Her second urge was to tell him to stop the car so she could get out. But she did neither. She swallowed it down and let it boil inside. The look on Steven's face—one that indicated he knew he had screwed up—was more than enough for her in that moment.

CHAPTER TWENTY TWO

Chloe wasted no time the following morning. Even though it was a Saturday, she sprang into action as if it were a typical workday. She even skipped out on her run again and managed to get ready for the day without uttering a word to Steven. He finally squeaked out a "Goodbye" from behind his cup of coffee as she walked out the front door, but she did not respond. She only closed the door hard and headed for her car, anxious to be away from him.

A small knot of dread started to form in her stomach as she finally made the decision: if Danielle wasn't going to speak to her, she'd get some information in other ways. She drove toward Danielle's apartment, that knot growing tighter and tighter with each mile. As she drove, she started to wonder at what point a case became too personal for an agent. Surely she was already over that line. She supposed Greene would have to sit her down at some point and tell her that she could no longer be active on the case.

But until then, she figured she'd do what she could.

As she approached Danielle's door, Chloe pulled out the small lock pick kit she had "borrowed" from her earlier days in the academy. It wasn't necessarily stealing, as it and various other resources were accessible to all agents in the skills labs. Without the proper guidance or instruction, though, what she was about to do would be heavily frowned upon.

It took her about ten seconds with the lock pick kit to get Danielle's door open. When she stepped inside, she closed the door quietly behind her, as if she knew she really shouldn't be there. She stood by the door and looked around. She wasn't even sure what she was looking for. She knew the bureau had already taken Danielle's laptop. They'd want to check her emails and all other digital communications with Martin.

She slowly walked a circuit around the apartment. She looked over her sister's belongings, realizing that she was in many ways the same young woman she had grown up with. The movie collection looked the same, the music collection looked the same, even the two shirts strewn on the couch with band names looked the same.

She walked into the kitchen, glad to see the prescription bottle gone and with Danielle. Feeling like a traitor, she started to snoop through her drawers and cabinets. She wasn't sure what she was looking for, exactly. When she found the kitchen not helpful, she walked into Danielle's bedroom. It was surprisingly neat. Then again, there was very little to be untidy; there was her bed (sloppily made), a single dresser, a bedside table, and a dirty clothes basket that was overflowing with mostly black clothes.

What the hell am I looking for?

She didn't know. She checked the bedroom closet and found nothing but a few boxes of old paperback books and a smattering of dressier clothes that probably never got worn. She also found nothing in the bathroom, though she did see an unopened pregnancy test kit which, she supposed, spoke volumes about Danielle's promiscuity.

When she walked back out into the living room, her eyes fell on the old roll-top desk that their grandmother had owned. It sat against the wall between the kitchen and the living room. When they had been much younger, Danielle had always been fixated on the roll top. She used it to play school, to do her homework, to sketch and doodle. It had seemed fitting that Danielle had taken it when their grandmother had passed away.

Chloe ran her hands along the curved portion that rolled up and down. She smiled at the memories it brought to the surface of her mind. Slowly, she lifted the roll-top to reveal the desk underneath. There, she saw scattered correspondence items: envelopes, stamps, loose-leaf paper, pens. There was nothing useful like an address book or a check register. Chloe frowned and started to roll the top back down.

But then she saw the few papers tucked in the back, behind a box of envelopes. They were very clearly hidden with some intention—the sort of thing you wanted to keep but not in plain sight. Chloe dug them out and found seven notes.

She read them and her heart seemed to stop beating for a moment. They were all short, most not even a sentence in length. They were also written in a very steady hand, all on what appeared to be sketchbook paper. They had apparently all come in envelopes that looked almost elegant. There were no addresses on the envelopes, neither of the sender nor the recipient. She read them one by one and, although they made her incredibly uneasy, they also instilled a hope that these might be the start of getting Danielle out of custody.

Reading over them, she tried to find some meaning or purpose behind them.

You'll never change, will you?

Tell anyone about these letters and I'll kill you. Stop looking into the past.

The guy you brought home last night is probably married. Slut.

Aren't you ashamed of what you've become? You should be dead, like your mother.

Does it hurt worse to be a whore or a failure?

YOU'RE ONLY GOING TO MAKE IT WORSE.

Kill him or I will.

The last one was clearly the most alarming. Was Martin the *him*? And if so, just who in the hell was delivering these letters? Chloe read them all again, returning each one to its envelope. When she was done with them, she held them closely to her side and carried them out of the apartment.

She felt like she'd discovered something important. Now the problem would be getting Danielle to speak with her. Chloe figured that if Danielle knew who was sending the letters, they might know who had really killed Martin.

It could have been her, some stubborn and logical part of her mind said as she returned to her car. But as she placed the letters on the seat, she knew better.

Knowing the messages those letters contained, she almost felt like the real killer was sitting right there beside her. And for some reason, they had something against Danielle.

But what? And why?

Chloe didn't know. But she sure as hell intended to find out.

***

She placed a call to Agent Greene before she was even out of the Lavender Hills subdivision. He answered right away, as he always did, and already sounded like the day had taken it out of him.

"You sound beat," she told him.

"No, I'm good. I've just been inundated with a shit-ton of information in the last half an hour. And you may find some of it extremely relevant, actually. Although I don't know if you would consider it good news or bad news."

"Is it about Danielle?"

"It is. She's fine…but they've transferred her. They've taken her to Riverside Correctional. As of about five o'clock this morning, she's officially being held in a prison."

"But she hasn't even been convicted yet!"

"True. But her alibis are so thin, Chloe. And the hair…that's the nail in the coffin. Her hair on the body…it was hers. She did submit to a DNA test and the hair came back as hers."

"Shit…"

"I think she'd probably speak with you now. I literally just got off the phone with one of the guys at Riverside. She's only been there for a little while, but she seems docile and cooperative from what he's telling me."

"I need to try…"

"I figured. I told them there was a good chance that I'd be sending an intern from the bureau to speak with her. I gave them your name and they obviously picked up on the last name matching. They're not thrilled with the idea, but they're going to allow it since she technically hasn't been convicted yet."

"Thanks, Agent Greene."

"Don't thank me yet. As an intern, this is going to be heavy. I honestly don't expect you to successfully separate the personal from the professional."

"It won't be a problem. I'll meet you at HQ after I've talked to her."

"Great," he said with a smile in his voice. "I'll see you then."

Chloe ended the call and increased her speed. Thinking of Danielle in prison was the equivalent of someone reaching into her past and breaking apart some of the better memories. She needed to speak to Danielle to learn *everything* she knew—to get to the bottom of the threatening letters she had found.

And then she was going to have to find who wrote them if she intended to clear her sister's name.

***

The officers greeted her warmly and wasted no time guiding her down the corridors of Riverside Correctional. At once, Chloe's alarms started going off. She heard someone screaming further off in the building. She could also hear another woman muttering something from somewhere close by, sounds of hateful gibberish.

And her sister was here. God help her.

The officers handed Chloe off to a guard who walked her down a final hall and then unlocked the door to a small room. It was decorated with only a small conference table and three chairs. Danielle was occupying one of the chairs. She looked up at Chloe as she entered and managed something that was supposed to be a smile.

Danielle didn't look as bad as Chloe had expected. She had been expecting to see a haggard woman, cried out and on the verge of losing her mind. Instead, Danielle simply looked tired. And because she always looked a little tired, it wasn't much of a difference in Chloe's eyes.

She also looked mad, though. Chloe supposed this was to be expected, given the way the last forty-eight hours of her life had gone.

"Danielle...I'm so sorry," Chloe said. "How are you doing?" Chloe had fully expected a hug at the very least. But Danielle remained seated and shook her head. She was clearly still very pissed off. When she spoke, her voice sounded rough and far away. "Not great, Chloe."

"I've been trying to figure out how—"

"I'm not expecting you to save the day," Danielle said. "I know there's only so much you can do. And you know what? When these men that have been interrogating me break down the way the case looks...I can understand why you thought it was me. It *does* sound bad. And I didn't help matters by sinking the damn car. I don't blame you for thinking it was me."

"You're right about me not being able to do much," Chloe said. "But the agent that is overseeing me is being very cooperative and understanding. He let me go look around your apartment for anything I could find. And I found the letters, Danielle...the threatening letters that came in the unaddressed envelopes."

Danielle said nothing; she looked at the surface of the table like a child being scolded by a concerned parent.

"Why didn't you tell me about them?" Chloe asked.

"Well, you read them. The one that said I'd be killed if I told anyone made me very hesitant to share that information. Besides...what the hell was I going to tell you? I don't know who is sending them and they come at random times. But this last one...they apparently knew I was dating Martin and...Chloe, do you really think they killed him?"

"It seems to point in that direction but it also seems a little too perfect. Like a setup."

"Chloe…I swear to you that I did not kill him. I understand how what I did to the car makes it look that way but you have to believe me."

"I do. But I have to tell you that the case against you is a strong one. The fingerprint and the hair basically nailed you. How did it get there if you didn't do it? The fingerprint makes sense, but not the hair."

"I just don't know," she said. "But I was in that car quite a few times. I don't think it's such a stretch to think that at some point, one of my loose hairs got caught on his clothes or his arm or something."

Chloe had considered the very same things but knew that it would all seem very flimsy in court. What made it harder was even this two-minute visit had confirmed Danielle's innocence in Chloe's mind. Again, though, the heart and gut instinct of a sister wasn't going to hold up in court, either.

"How is it here?" Chloe asked. "Do you feel safe, at least?"

"Well, they've got me in a holding cell at the end of the building away from gen pop. But they're refusing to even acknowledge my meds. I have no idea where they are…probably with my personal belongings. I just feel trapped…which I guess is the whole point of a prison, right?"

The little joke fell flat. Chloe tried to keep her own emotions in check. After all, what sense did it make for her to feel helpless when it was, in fact, Danielle who needed all of the help?

"I'll do what I can to make sure you get your meds. And I swear to you that I'll do everything I can to find out who really killed Martin. I don't know how long you'll be in holding until they actually charge you…"

The door to the room opened behind them and a tall man with completely gray hair and an expensive suit stepped in.

"My lawyer," Danielle said. "State appointed."

"That's right," the man said, stepping forward and offering his hand. "Pete Jackson. I'll be working with Danielle and seeing what we can do to prevent this charge from sticking. I take it you're the sister she's mentioned?"

"I am. Agent Chloe Fine." Of course, she wasn't quite an agent yet, but this state-appointed lawyer didn't need to know that.

"Well, as the agent trying to free her, *and* the sister, I think it's important that you know this is not looking good. That fingerprint—"

"On the key, yes," Chloe said. "Are her prints anywhere on Martin's body?" she asked defensively.

"No, but the—"

"And has anyone found a murder weapon yet?"

"No," Jackson said, seeing where this was going.

"Then I'd kindly appreciate it if you wouldn't speak about your client as if the verdict has already been pinned on her. Maybe do your job a bit better."

"Of course I will try my best to reach an innocent verdict," Jackson said. "But you have to understand that based on what I'm working with, I have to look at where the evidence is pointing. And right now, it's pointing towards a lifetime sentence for second-degree murder. In the end, we may have to strike a plea bargain. I'm just trying to prepare Danielle for what she can potentially expect."

As if the words had placed some sort of spell on Danielle, she let out a gasping sort of moan the moment the sentence was over. Chloe had never heard such a sound come from Danielle, and it wrecked her. She cast a hateful look toward Jackson. He sighed and slowly backed out of the room, quietly closing the door behind him.

It was then that Danielle got out of her chair and rushed over to Chloe. The sisters embraced in a way they hadn't since childhood, in a way that brought back fun summer days as well as nights plagued with bad dreams. Chloe had to choke back her own little cry of sorrow as she wrapped Danielle in her arms.

"I want to tell you it's going to be okay, but I can't do that right now," Chloe said.

"I know," Danielle said into her ear. "And that's okay. It's not your job."

But Chloe disagreed. If she was going to pave her own way as an agent, what better way than breaking this case open—than rescuing her sister when it seemed there was an ironclad case against her?

If she was going to be an agent worth a damn, maybe it *was* her job.

CHAPTER TWENTY THREE

Of the two Fine sisters, Chloe was absolutely the more sentimental and emotional. But there comes a time when sentiment and emotion will only get you so far. It was very rare that they got results. It was this mindset that had Chloe leaving Riverside Correctional just fifteen minutes after she'd arrived. With tears still drying on the side of her face, she went back to HQ. She blasted right by her office and even neglected to check in with Greene. She went straight for the lab that was provided for the interns, just off of the primary lab for the field agents. Being a Saturday, it was very quiet in the lab, giving her the silence and space she needed to do her best thinking.

She took the letters from Danielle's apartment out of her laptop bag and started doing her best to come up with some sort of an answer. She used one of the basic evidence kits to study the letters and the envelopes closer. She had only ever done this once before in a real-life situation, helping to pull prints from a crowbar earlier in the year. Still, she'd gone through these motions more than a dozen times in the course of her training and was comfortable enough to be working it alone.

She started off by carefully dusting them for prints. She dusted the letters themselves first and then the envelopes. The powder revealed several fingerprints, all of which could easily belong to Danielle. She scanned the prints and ran them through the system. As she waited for results—which could take anywhere from ten minutes to two hours—she looked over the letters again. Was there some sort of symbolism in them, maybe even clues as to the identity of the writer?

She saw nothing that jumped out at her and decided it was just the deranged notes of someone with a very serious mental issue.

She then pulled out her laptop and pulled up the digital files that had been accumulated so far for the murder of Martin Shields. She found fairly detailed reports, including photographs of the car, the lake area, and the body. She found herself drawn to the pictures that showed the stab wounds, completely unable to imagine Danielle viciously ramming a knife into someone's chest.

It seemed absolutely impossible to her.

But she admitted to driving the car into the lake, she thought. *Really, how much more of a mental leap is it between doing something like that and seriously considering the act of putting a knife in someone's heart?*

"No," she said into the empty room.

Danielle didn't do this. We may feel like strangers sometimes, but I know her, dammit.

She handled the enveloped again, her hands secured in gloves. She checked the flaps and the sticker on the tapered edge of it. She looked at the underside of the flap, looking for any slight tears or gumming...any evidence that someone might have licked the envelope to close it. But she saw nothing of the sort. The writer had been careful there, too, using the sticker to close the envelope rather than providing a possible sample of their DNA by licking it.

As she tidied the letters up into a neat pile, the results from the fingerprints came back. She read over the results, not at all surprised by them.

The only prints on the envelopes and the letters were Danielle's. Of course she'd handled them. There was no way in hell she'd ever think her fingerprints would be lifted off of it in relation to a murder investigation one day.

Chloe let out a curse and slammed her hand down on the table. She was angry and frightened, two emotions that did not go well together. Not knowing what else to do and feeling very much like a kid who had gotten in over her head, she picked up her phone and placed a call to Greene.

"Hey, Fine," he said. "How's your sister?"

"Scared shitless," Chloe said. "And with good reason. Agent Greene...I know you don't know me very well at all but I need you to trust me. My sister did not do this. And I don't know how to explain it to you other than a sister's intuition. I *know* her. She didn't do this."

"Then you need to prove it. I want you to think like an agent...like you're no longer an intern but an actual field agent. If you wanted to prove her innocence, what's the most surefire way to do it?"

"I'd need to find something that links someone else to the scene," she said. She was vaguely aware that Greene was currently about as strict as he had ever been with her—but still helpful. She wondered if he had formed his own opinions about Danielle and the case.

"Good thinking. Now how would you do that?"

"Well, I'd need to revisit the scene. But the car's gone now. And by the time I get permission to look inside of it—assuming it's already at the scrap yard—Danielle would probably be convicted. So…"

She stopped, thinking. *So what? What would the next step be?*

It came to her slowly and it truly did make her feel like she was a huge step beyond an intern. "Agent Greene, where are you right now?"

"In town, about to interview a witness to a B and E. Why?"

"How soon can you meet me at the morgue?"

"And why would I want to do that?" Greene asked in a playfully mocking tone that let her know exactly why he'd want to do that.

"Because I need to get a look at the body."

"Good work, Fine. And yes…I can meet you there in an hour."

CHAPTER TWENTY FOUR

Chloe had been required to undergo what the students had referred to as "morgue time" during her second year of classes, mostly to get used to the idea of having to look over dead bodies for evidence and clues. It had been an uncomfortable experience, but it hadn't really bothered her.

What she discovered when she met Greene at the morgue to look over Martin's body was that those classes were one thing—and being up close and personal with a freshly dead body—one she had recently met while still alive, at that—was a completely different situation. When she and Greene were granted access to the examination room, everything in the world seemed to go still and quiet. She looked over the body, completely nude and exposed to the halogen lights overhead.

The stab wounds had been slightly cleaned but not yet completely tidied up. Chloe could now see the marks quite clearly. She was surprised how almost *fake* they seemed. But it was all too real…and she was going to have to get used to it.

"Tell me what you're looking for," Greene said, clearly quizzing her.

"Any signs of a struggle other than the stab wounds," she said. "Bruising, abrasions, things like that."

"And why would those be of any interest to us?"

"They'd be a very good source for fingerprints."

"Indeed. Remember that we also have his clothes being scoured for prints and hairs as well. So far, nothing."

Greene stood back and let her examine the body. The only thing out of the ordinary she could find was a small bruise between the neck and the base of the shoulder. It was the kind that could have come from anything, small and light.

"Tell me what you're thinking as you process," Greene said. "Like if you were recording your notes."

"Nothing of interest right away," she said. "Though the fact that the wounds are from the front indicates a bigger chance of there being a struggle. That being said, I've looked at the wrists and the backs of the hands for any sign of a fight. Seeing that there are none leads me to believe that the murderer was right there with him when it happened. I doubt the killer took him by surprise. Therefore, the killer was likely someone he trusted."

Someone like Danielle, she thought.

She crossed her arms and gave it some more thought. "Of course, there could have still been a struggle, just a very bad one. But I've seen Martin move. He moves like someone with some training…perhaps a boxer or mixed martial artist. The headlock he put Steven into was a pro one. So perhaps he struck a defensive pose from his training to try to ward off an attack—but was just too late."

She leaned in and checked his hands again. She still saw nothing on them to indicate that he had been involved in a recent struggle. She did, however, find dirt beneath his fingernails. And it appeared to be fresh.

"I've got some dirt under the fingernails here," she said.

She leaned in closer as Greene selected a drawer to his right and fished around inside. "We technically aren't allowed to do this…" he said, but took something out of the drawer anyway. It was a simple scraping device, about the thickness of a sheet of thin cardboard but with the appearance of a scalpel.

Chloe used this to scrape some of the dirt out from beneath Martin's fingernails. It was tightly compacted but even from the few grains that fell onto the exam table, she could tell that there was also some blood mixed in with it.

"Looks to be some blood mixed in with the dirt," she said. "Could be his own, but if he tried to defend himself at all, it could also be the killer's."

"Good work," Greene said. "I'll head out and get someone to bag this up. I'll make it a priority and we should have results back from that blood within four to six hours."

The idea of it was exciting but she then realized that it could come back as Danielle's blood. And if that were the case, she would have been working this entire time to do nothing more than solidify Danielle's prison term.

Apparently, this realization showed on her face. Greene paused at the door and hesitated. "You sure you don't want to sit this one out?"

"I'm sure. Even if…well, even if the results come back with bad news, at least I'll know. And if it's her then I have to know why. I have to understand."

120

"With all due respect," Greene said, "that's something you need to let go of. Because in my experience, it's sometimes better that we don't understand why people kill."

He left the room, leaving Chloe to ruminate on that. And even as she did, one solid certainty floated through her mind.

It's not Danielle. It can't be…

***

Chloe was back in the records room at HQ, going over the most recent report on the crime scene at the lake, when the door flew open. Two men walked inside, only one of whom she knew. Greene stood beside the other man, dwarfed by his size. The other man was tall and built like a pro wrestler, an attribute that was evident even beneath his suit. Chloe had seen him before and knew who he was, though she had never actually spoken with him.

Director L.J. Johnson took a seat directly across from Chloe, leaving Greene to stand. Johnson looked across the table at her with an expression that was hard to read. He looked from Chloe to the records, and then back to Chloe.

"I assume Agent Greene told you about our program to slowly allow some of our interns to get closer to the action, correct?" Johnson asked.

"Yes, sir."

"I stand by the decision but I will admit wholeheartedly that it irritated the eternal piss out of me when I discovered that you and Agent Greene had submitted another DNA test in this Martin Shields case. I called up Greene and chewed him out and fully planned to call you and ask who the hell you thought you were, too. After all, this isn't even a bureau case. The locals out there near Pinecrest are doing me a favor because of your connection to the thing. So I was pissed. But then the results came back and I'll be damned if I wasn't proven wrong."

"It's not Danielle Fine's blood, is it?" Chloe asked.

"No, it's not. The results came back for a man named Alan Short. And that is information that we are keeping to ourselves. When I leave this room, I'm dedicating two agents to tracking this man down. I am then going to personally push the paperwork that will lead to your sister's release. However…you have to be realistic about this. She is still a suspect until Alan Short is caught. She is still not to leave the state and must agree to further questioning."

"Of course," Chloe said. "Thank you."

"No, thank *you*. Impressive work, Fine. I look forward to working with you when you're no longer an intern. Agent Greene, keep up the good work on working with her."

With that, Johnson got to his feet and left the room. Greene gave Chloe a *can-you-believe-that* sort of look.

"One thing I noticed," Chloe said, "was that he's assigned other agents to bring this guy in. I feel like I've been demoted."

"Hey, you can't expect the entire world. Seriously...the fact that he came in to congratulate you is huge. So take that and your sister's presumed innocence as a victory. I'll keep you posted on progress in the Alan Short investigation. If he's a local, I imagine we'll have him in custody within forty-eight hours."

"That's great," Chloe said, feeling the weight come off of her chest right away.

"You know, she *will* probably be charged with *something*. Ditching his car like that seems highly suspect. She's off for now...but I fully expect that there will be an ongoing investigation."

"That makes sense," Chloe said, still simply relieved that Danielle was no longer the primary suspect. "So now what do we do?"

"For this case? Nothing. You've done everything you could. I think maybe you should call it a day and head home. When Danielle is released, I imagine your days will be rather hectic. Like Director Johnson said...we're sitting on this for right now. Which means the media won't know anything substantial until Alan Short is caught."

"Can I tell Danielle the news?"

"Not yet. We have to wait until the paperwork is done. But if Director Johnson is on it, that will be done very soon. Seriously, Chloe. Go home. Good work today."

She got up from the table and tidied up the records she had been looking through. She was visibly trembling as she tried to absorb everything that had happened during the course of the day— most notably the last five minutes or so.

She'd potentially freed Danielle.

She had Director Johnson—a man who would eventually be her supervisor—already thanking her and congratulating her.

It looked like the future was bright. It looked like the dark past that has pushed her toward these moments was finally releasing her from its clutches.

But as she'd soon discover, the past had a way of sticking around and not only surprising you, but shaking any future plans into dust. It was proven in the form of the letters that had been delivered to Danielle, hinting that the past was never too far away.

But who sent them? Chloe wondered, the questioning itching at her. *And perhaps more importantly, why?*

CHAPTER TWENTY FIVE

Despite the tension that existed between them ever since the block party, Chloe and Steven had managed to remain civil. Chloe was still excited and pleased over the fact that her insights and work—with Greene's guidance—had helped to clear Danielle's name. She was so excited about it that when she found Steven on the couch, looking over his emails, she had every intention of jumping him. They'd not been physical for about a week—which seemed a shame since they had an entire house to break in.

That all came to a very cold stop when she arrived home and tried to share her news with him. She felt a little silly as she did it, beaming and feeling as if she was bragging. She started with finding the blood under Martin's fingernails and then the brief meeting with Director Johnson. But even before she told him the full details of Danielle's eventual release, it was clear that he wasn't going to be sharing in her joy.

"Hold on," Steven said. There appeared to be equal measures of fascination and disgust on his face. "You mean to tell me that you were right there, in the room with Martin's corpse?"

"Yes. I told you...I'm part of an experimental program that gives interns more freedom and responsibilities."

"Yes, I know that," he spat. "But you were right there with the body...and you had no problem still defending her?"

"No, I didn't," she said, instantly getting defensive. "No matter your feelings about Danielle, even your contempt can't overrule DNA evidence. Sorry her freedom is going to screw with your mom's perfect image for our wedding."

"I didn't say that."

"You didn't have to. It's been on your mind since the first time your mother complained about her."

"Chloe, that's not fair...or accurate."

"Well, that's good to know. Because when she is released tomorrow, she can't go back to her apartment. It's too risky and there will be media everywhere. So I want her to come back here for a few days."

"What?" Steven asked, incredulous. "Are you out of your mind?"

"No. What would be your problem with it?" She knew she had an argument on her hands now but she was digging her heels in. She wasn't worried about what Sally Brennan thought anymore. This was her sister's future on the line now. Sally could take her wedding money and shove it for all Chloe cared.

"There would be a convicted murderer in our house!"

"No...not convicted. Did you miss the part where I said she was being released?"

"And you think that matters?" Steven asked, yelling now. "Freed or not, this will stick with her. For years—maybe even her whole life."

"And how does that affect you, exactly?"

"Chloe...you're not thinking clearly. I get it. She's your sister. But she can't stay here."

"Well, she *is* staying here. I'm sorry but it's not open for discussion."

He looked at her as if he had no idea who he was speaking with. And what pissed her off more than anything was that she knew he was worried what his parents would think. That was the only reason he was being so stubborn.

"You said this new blood sample proves someone else was involved," he said quietly. "Until I hear otherwise, she could have still been responsible. She could still be a murderer."

"You want her to be, don't you? Then it'll get her out of your hair. And your mother's."

"You sound insane," he said, his voice still low and calm now. "And you know what? My folks have been trying to get me to see it for a while now."

"See what, Steven?"

"Your loyalty to your sister, no matter what. I know you two have been through some shit, but this is crazy. And Chloe...maybe this is a mistake. The engagement, the wedding. They were right, I think...we're not right for each other."

"Because I am loyal to my sister?" she asked. She wasn't hurt so much as she was confused and livid.

"Because there's just too much baggage there. And yes...partly because you'll constantly choose your delusional sister over me. And if that's the way it's going to be during our marriage, I want no part of it."

So it's finally come to this, Chloe thought. *He's essentially asking me to choose between him and Danielle.*

She loved him. She had no qualms with admitting that.

But there was an image of her sister, nearly catatonic while she sat on those apartment steps with a cop by their side. She remembered that day clearly and knew that no matter what life dealt them, she would always see her sister as that little girl. And she would do everything she could do protect her.

"I'm sorry, Steven," she said. "I'm not going to cut Danielle out of my life."

Without missing a beat, Steven said: "Then the wedding is off."

With that, he turned his back and headed for the door. There was no goodbye kiss, no hug, and barely even any eye contact. He went straight for the door and slammed it hard when he made his way out.

Chloe stood there, dumfounded. Her day had gone from the highest of highs to the lowest of lows in less than ten minutes. And all she was left with was this big house, now empty except for her. She looked slowly around the living room, taking in the absurdity of it all, before sinking to her knees and crying.

She was no stranger to weeping; she'd done plenty of it in the weeks following her mother's death and then again at the age of seventeen when the sense of not having a mother had really started to sink in as she ventured into the college years. But this weeping was some something new, something physically painful that seemed to grow inside of her stomach.

She wept on the couch, wanting to stop and get control but also knowing that it would be best to just let it all out. And when she thought of Danielle and the impossible situation *she* was in, she cried even harder—a sound that came back to her in small echoes that the large house sent right back to her.

CHAPTER TWENTY SIX

Sleep was incredibly fragmented that night. There were some moments where the knowledge that Danielle would be freed tomorrow had her excited and unable to sleep. Then another minute would pass and she would start to feel the weight of Steven leaving her all over again. It was a bold move and since Steven was not known for bold moves, she fully expected him to return at some point that night.

But he never showed up.

At some point, she managed to fall into something similar to a deep sleep but it did not last long. She received a text message at 5:35. She retrieved her phone from the bedside table without having much time to ruminate on the empty side of the bed behind her. With sleep-blurred eyes, she saw Greene's name on the display. The message read:

Paperwork will be approved by 8 this morning. We've already started getting things approved for you to be there to pick her up. Beware...the media will be there, too. I'll be there to assist.

With this news, any further sleep was out of the question. She got out of bed, put the coffee on, and took a shower while it percolated. After getting dressed and grabbing a quick breakfast of toast and oatmeal, she headed out. She figured she'd get there a little earlier than eight but she honestly wasn't too worried about that.

When she stepped out of her front door, there were several cars and two news vans parked on the side of the street. As she hurried to her car, the news crews also hurried forward. They came across the lawn as if they owned the place, their cameras and microphones at the ready.

"Are you absolutely certain your sister is innocent?" one reporter asked.

"Are you afraid of how this turn of events might hurt your career if it turns out Danielle was involved in any way?" another asked.

She cast her face toward the ground, refusing to even give them the privilege of filming her face. She got into her car and backed out quickly, nearly clipping a cameraman with the back end of her car.

If they're already at my house, she thought, *it's bound to be much worse at the jail.*

She drove quickly out of Lavender Hills, already spotting a few curious and nosy neighbors on their porches as the news vans gave chase. As she made it out of the neighborhood and onto the highway, she wondered if it was possible that any of her neighbors somehow already knew that Steven was gone.

These neighbors of hers—the women in particular—seemed to have a knack for knowing certain things. Why would her private argument with her fiancé yesterday afternoon be any different?

She couldn't help but feel a little sting of guilt. Maybe she *had* been too demanding. Maybe her absolute refusal to listen to his side when she'd told him that Danielle was going to be staying at the house had been out of line. It was, after all, partly his house.

But no...she refused to feel guilty. Steven and his parents had practically marked Danielle as a black sheep ever since she and Steven had started seriously dating. If that was the kind of people they were, maybe she really *didn't* need Steven and that sort of negativity in her life.

If she had to ride out this situation knowing that she had ultimately chosen her sister over a life with Steven, she was fine with that. It stung, but she could live with it and feel that she had made the right decision.

That, of course, led her to thinking of how Danielle had gotten into this mess in the first place. Her dating Martin wasn't all that peculiar, but the fact that someone had placed evidence pointing toward her on his body *was.*

She knew that she had basically been told to stay off of the pending case—that more seasoned agents were handling it now. But she couldn't help but wonder who Alan Short was and what his connection to Danielle might be. Perhaps Greene would stand true to his word and keep her updated. She had no reason to assume any different.

It took her half an hour to get to Riverside Correctional. She arrived twenty minutes early but she thought that was for the best. When she arrived, the parking lot and the street were swarming with television newscasters—some local and some on a national level. She realized that the death of Martin Shields itself was not newsworthy. But when you threw in a car backed into a lake and the possibility of planted evidence, it became even juicier. And if the news was running with the Alan Short story, it would be almost headline worthy while Short was searched for.

She toyed with the idea of simply sitting in her car and waiting for Greene to arrive but saw that it would do no good. Even before she had parked her car, reporters came rushing forward. Doing her best to outpace them, Chloe opened her car door and again walked with her head down.

More questions came hurling toward her and this time she did respond. She kept repeating *"No comment, no comment."* It was chilling and infuriating to hear so many people referring to her sister as a murderer. She had to make a great effort to not lash out at every misinformed question as the questions become more barbed the closer she got to the jail.

Apparently, a good Samaritan cop saw what was happening on his way into the building. He came rushing over and stood in front of her with his arms splayed and led her through the growing melee of reporters and cameramen.

"You will all back up and give Ms. Fine some room. Anyone even accidentally touches her, you'll be looking at fines. Got it?"

This pushed the tide of people back somewhat but not enough to make Chloe comfortable. She followed the cop to the building, where he ushered her in through the doors and into the front lobby. Once inside, she noticed that a few people were looking curiously at her—the receptionist, a few officers, a woman waiting in a chair in the lobby.

"Agent Fine," the cop said, "I'm Officer Wright. Sorry you had to deal with that."

"It is what it is," she said, barely noticing that he had referred to her as *Agent.* "They were outside of my home, too."

"Jesus," Wright said. "Anyway, I assume you're here for your sister?"

"I am."

"Let me see what I can do to get things rolling," Wright said.

Chloe spent the next ten minutes showing her badge to people and signing forms. As she was signing what she was told would be the last one while standing by a little kiosk that separated the central building from an expansive hallway, another officer came up beside her. Agent Greene was with him and he looked angry.

"Damned vultures are roosting outside," he said. "How did you make it in without cold-cocking one?"

"Oh, it took some effort."

The uniformed officer who had given Chloe the last form looked it over, stamped it, and then nodded. "You're good to go, Ms. Fine."

Chloe and Agent Greene were buzzed in through the door that led into the hallway. There was only one door along this hallway and as they stepped into the hall, it was opening. An armed guard walked out, ushering Danielle ahead of him.

Her arms were not cuffed and she was dressed in the same clothes she'd been wearing when she had been brought in. It had only been two days but something about this seemed barbaric to Chloe.

Danielle came quickly toward her and when she threw her arms around her, Chloe could hardly believe it. When she returned the embrace, Danielle felt as light as a feather. She was also trembling—maybe crying. Chloe wanted to know for sure but also did not want to embarrass Danielle, as she knew shows of emotion were not common for her.

So she let it go and, for the moment, simply held her sister in her arms.

And she knew in that moment that while she'd miss Steven for quite some time, she had absolutely made the right decision.

***

The bureau had not seen the sense in devoting agents to escorting Chloe and Danielle back to Pinecrest. Instead, two cops tailed them into Pinecrest where they were then handed off to two Pinecrest PD patrol cars. Those patrol cars followed them into Lavender Hills and then parked alongside the curb outside of Chloe's house. She pulled her own car into the driveway and parked, taking note of the news crews. There were more of them now—four from her count—but they seemed a little more hesitant to come after her with the cops' cars parked in front of the house.

The sisters hurried inside. Chloe could hear the clicking of phones and actual cameras as well as the murmurs of reporters as they made notes and spoke to television audiences.

"When I was a teenager," Danielle said, "I thought about learning to play the guitar. I figured I'd be a Liz Phair or Joan Jett or something. I thought it would be cool to have people with cameras following me around. I now realize what a stupid fucking dream that was."

Chloe couldn't help but laugh. They sat down on the couch together and it was clear that they didn't quite know how to behave around one another.

"So, Steven left," Chloe said as if she was commenting on the weather.

"What? When?"

"Last night. We had an argument and he left."

"Was it about me?"

"Partly," Chloe said.

"Chloe, I'm so sorry. It's my fault. You want me to call him and explain—"

"God, no! Honestly, it's a blessing, I think. His parents are insufferable and treat him like Jesus Christ."

Danielle shrugged and sank into the couch. "I'm sad for you but I'd be lying if I said I'm going to miss him. So…no wedding?"

"Doesn't look like it. Turns out you won't have to wear that bridesmaid dress after all."

"This day just keeps getting better and better," Danielle said with a wry smile.

Chloe got up and went into the kitchen to make them some lunch. As childish as it seemed, she used the mustard that Steven always claimed was *his* mustard on their sandwiches. As she put them together, Danielle turned the television on in the living room. She flipped through the channels, skimming the sorry excuse for early afternoon programming before settling on a local news program.

They both froze for a moment when they saw footage of them exiting Riverside Correctional. Their heads were down as they were ushered out by four policemen. She saw Agent Greene bringing up the rear, shooting scouring glances at the reporters that trailed them. Danielle turned it up and they both listened to the report.

"….says that while the evidence is fairly solid, new findings in the case indicate that other parties were involved. These new findings aren't quite enough to exonerate Danielle Fine, but they are enough to apparently release her from custody. Officials are stating that the new findings are sensitive and not yet being fully revealed to the public due to the nature of the investigation. As for now, though, Danielle Fine remains the only suspect in the public's eye. When asked for comment, Baltimore City PD stated that Fine has agreed to remain cooperative in regards to questioning and other details of the investigation. Here, we see her leaving Riverside with her sister, up-and-coming FBI agent Chloe Fine. We've recently discovered that these two sisters have been through quite a lot, possibly even having witnessed the death of their mother at the hands of their father. We can't be—"

"And screw you, too," Danielle said, turning the television off. "I look like shit on TV."

"You haven't slept in nearly two days," Chloe pointed out. "Of course you're going to look tired."

"But not guilty, hopefully." She paused here as Chloe brought the sandwiches and some chips into the living room. "So what do you know about this Alan Short guy?"

"Nothing. You?"

"Same. And listen...I know you were just doing your job the whole time. And because of my idiot move of dropping that car in the lake, I know I looked guilty. It means a lot to me that you managed to look past that and not give up. It really does. No one has ever *not* given up on me, you know?"

Chloe didn't want to verbally confirm this, so she just nodded. "So, you don't know Alan Short. But can you think of anyone who might want you framed for Martin's death?"

Danielle sighed and looked at her sandwich—anything not to meet Chloe's eyes. "I don't know any one person," she replied. "But I should probably tell you about this one thing I've been keeping from you."

"What's that?" Chloe asked, a little spike of fear piercing her heart. Of course, she was pretty sure she knew what was coming. She was so sure that she went ahead and answered her own question. "Are you talking about those letters?"

"Yeah. And by the way, how did you say you found them?" Danielle asked.

"I went by your apartment after they arrested you. I wanted to see if I could find anything to free you. These letters...if there's even a remote chance that Alan Short wrote them—hell, even if there isn't a chance he wrote them—I feel like we need to submit them as evidence."

"You saw them all, right?" Danielle asked. "One of them says that if I go to anyone about them, they'd kill me. And now, after Martin turns up dead, I believe it more than ever. That last one...*Kill him or I will.* The 'him' was Martin, right?"

"We have no way of knowing that for sure."

"Seems a little wonky if it's not. The timing adds it all up as far as I'm concerned."

"When did you get the first one?" Chloe asked.

132

"About six months ago."

"And they'd just show up at random times?"

"Seemed like it," Danielle answered. "I've tried going back over my schedule for those six months to see if I could have done something to piss someone off. The worst I could come up with was turning men down at the bar."

"Well, what about less troublesome things? Have you gotten involved with new friends or people at work?"

"No. I don't have the patience for making friends, really. Although—funny enough, you'll love this—I did look into doing a book group."

"Did you join?"

"No. But it's pretty cool. I was looking through a few of things I had from Mom and found this book she had. *Different Seasons* by Stephen King. There was a little note inside of it with Mom's handwriting. They were reading it for a book club she was part of, right here in Pinecrest. I called the library and asked if they still did a book club and they said they did. So based on that, I almost joined. I even asked if there was any way to look into who might have been past members. I told them I was just doing some digging into my mother's history…and that was the truth, as dumb as it sounds. Just to know there was a book club she once belonged to, you know? Remember how she loved to read?"

"I do."

"Anyway, they said they had records of sign-up sheets but nothing any farther back than 2002."

"But you've got notes that prove that Mom was part of this book club?" Chloe asked.

"Yeah. But then the threatening notes started coming and I got a little distracted. I just never even thought about joining again."

"Any idea how much time passed between the call to the library and the notes showing up?"

"I don't know for sure. Two weeks? Maybe three."

There was a lackluster tone in her voice that made Chloe want to cringe. Danielle looked tired and, despite being recently freed from prison, infinitely sad. Chloe recognized the signs of depression from Danielle's earlier years.

God, we can't go back to that, she thought.

"And what did you say about the timing adding it all up for you?" Chloe asked with a bit of sarcasm.

"Yeah, but a book club? You thinking some sinister librarian has it out for me because I didn't join?"

"No. But did you specifically mention Mom?"

"Yeah."

Chloe wasn't sure what it all meant—or of it meant anything at all.

But it was sure as hell worth looking into. Apparently, Danielle felt this, too. The living room fell into silence as both women turned their attention to the windows, keeping an eye on the media presence outside.

CHAPTER TWENTY SEVEN

The news headlines didn't get any better. Reporters were now digging into the sordid history of their parents, painting Danielle as a victim of a childhood with no real parents. They had also uncovered a public intoxication charge from Danielle's past and were harping on that now as well.

Chloe was again alarmed that Danielle was starting to sink into some sort of vague depression. She was no longer trying to make light of things and the woman who had given her a hug at Riverside Correctional that morning seemed to have gone into hiding. That brooding little girl Chloe had grown up lurked right behind the surface, ready to slink out of hiding and take up residence.

They had sunk into silence after the talk about the book club, but it was a silence that Chloe broke after less than ten minutes. She thought she had picked up a very thin trail, one that might actually not even be there at all. But she had to try.

"Danielle, do you remember the day Mom died when we were in the back of Grandma's car? I remember you saying that you knew Dad didn't do it. Do you still feel that way?"

"I do," she said in that same sleepy tone. It wasn't that she didn't care about the discussion but it was almost as if it was taking immense mental willpower to take part in it—another signal of her depression looming.

"Any reason why?"

"I don't know. I just always had this sense that he wasn't capable of it. If you think back about it, he never hit Mom. Never even raised his hand to her from what I can remember. If he had *anything* to do with it, it was an accident. I mean, she fell down the stairs. There was no weapon, nothing malicious, you know?"

Chloe was still slightly hung up on the timing of it all—of Danielle inquiring about her mother being part of a book club just a few weeks before those threatening notes started. And while Danielle wasn't quite ready to make the jump to believing that the letter writer had something to do with Martin's death, the notes certainly did seem ominous.

But if she followed that trail, no matter how broken it might be, it all led back to one place: their mother. The book club was such a

135

small thing and likely meant very little in the grand scheme of things. And Chloe knew that if she ventured down that trail, it would lead her toward looking into her mother's death and their father's incarceration—something she promised herself she would never do.

But now Danielle's name was being dragged through the mud. And if Chloe could make that stop by looking into their past, she figured it was necessary.

"Do you remember the cop that sat with us on the stoop?" Chloe asked, an idea suddenly springing to her mind.

Danielle smiled. "Yeah. Clarence Simmons, don't know why I remember his name. Big guy. Really nice. I remember that he looked almost as sad as we did the whole time he was there."

Chloe mulled over an idea for a moment. A slow anxiousness started to take shape in her stomach as the idea seemed more and more relevant. "Did he ever say anything to you that afternoon?" Chloe asked.

"Nothing in particular," Danielle said. "Just that it would be okay. He kept saying that over and over again. You know, it's funny…I didn't even piece it together until later…when I was going through that therapy nonsense right after it all happened. Did you know that he used to live next door to Amber Hayes?"

"Amber Hayes?" Chloe asked. She knew the name but wasn't sure why.

"Yeah. That girl that always had that stupid bike with the annoying bell, driving it everywhere and *ding ding ding.*"

"Oh God, yeah, I remember. Hold on…she lived like what…maybe three blocks away from the apartment, right?"

"Something like that," Danielle said.

"You have any idea where she lives now?"

"I do, actually. She tried chatting me up on Facebook Messenger a while back. She's living somewhere in New York, I think."

"You happen to have her number?"

Danielle rolled her eyes and pulled out her phone. "Well, I have the number of her business. She gave it to me, thinking for some reason I might need advertising services…why, I have no idea."

Danielle found the number and gave it to Chloe. Chloe wasted no time calling the number. She knew she was working with a long shot, but it was one worth taking. The phone rang three times in her ear before it was answered.

"Helmsley Ad Services, this is Amber."

"Amber, hi. This is Chloe Fine. Do you remember me?"

There was a brief silence on the other end, broken by a response that was too theatrical to be sincere. "Yes! My God, how are you? I've seen the news…how is Danielle?"

"She's scared, but good. She was just mentioning how you guys had chatted not too long ago."

"Yeah! I came to Pinecrest to see my folks about a month ago. I had been hoping to meet up with her."

"Look, Amber, I hate to be short with you, but I was hoping you could help me find an address. Do you remember the man you guys used to live next door to back here in Pinecrest? He was a policeman. Clarence Simmons."

Amber laughed and when she responded, there was legitimate joy in her voice. "Oh yes indeed. Mr. Simmons was so sweet. He and my father still talk. They met each other for a fishing trip last summer, I believe."

"Is he still in Pinecrest?" Chloe asked.

"No. He moved about eight years ago, I think. Maybe longer than that. He moved to New Jersey."

"Do you have an address? Maybe your dad?"

"You know, I *do* have an address. He still sends me Christmas cards. If you give me a few minutes, I can shoot it your way."

"That would be excellent," Chloe said. "Thanks so much, Amber."

She ended the call and found Danielle looking at her with something like awe. "Is it really that easy for you to get information?"

"Not always. I think this is what people at the bureau call *a lucky break*. She has an address but needs to look for it."

Danielle went to the window and looked out. Chloe looked over her shoulder and saw that one other news van had showed up. A petite woman was speaking in front of a camera, angled to capture the entire house in the shot. Two police cars were parked behind it all, one officer standing out by the hood. He smoked a cigarette and glared at the circus.

They remained in the house, Chloe feeling like a prisoner. She got updates on the hunt for Alan Short via texts from Greene. They also kept tabs on Danielle's story on news stations and the Internet but it was only infuriating them.

The monotony broke around 4:30, when Amber called back. Chloe made this call quick, too, but not without expressing her gratitude. She wrote the address down and ended the call, feeling that she might actually be getting somewhere.

"Trenton, New Jersey," she said.

"Lucky for us," Danielle said. "He could have moved to California or something. That would make this a little tough, huh?"

"You can't come with me," Chloe said. "Until you are absolutely one hundred percent cleared in Martin's death, you can't leave town. If you want, I can ask Greene to keep tabs on you."

Looking depressed, Danielle shook her head. "No. I'm fine with just the rent-a-cops outside. When are you going?"

"I'll leave in the morning. No sense in driving out there during rush hour only to catch him at night."

"So a girls' night in, I take it?" Danielle asked.

Chloe was irritated that she was trying to make a joke of it. But she also knew her sister well enough to know that joking was how she handled stress. It had always been the case, even from the age of five or so. Whenever she made such sweeping jokes, it was a sure sign of stress or worry.

And Chloe supposed there was still plenty to worry about as of right now.

"Looks like it," she said with a smile.

"Sounds good. You get the wine and I'll find something on TV."

It was good to hear Danielle in her devil-may-care attitude again, even if it was mostly staged. Like Chloe, Danielle was also sensing something being pieced together and wasn't sure how to feel about having to revisit their past to make sense of it.

Still, Chloe selected a bottle of red from the small wine rack in the kitchen and poured two glasses. When she walked into the living room to deliver one to Danielle, she noted that yet another news crew had arrived on the scene.

This either meant that something new in the story was developing or it was just a slow news day.

Chloe was fine not knowing. She looked away from the window and watched as Danielle scrolled through Netflix for something to watch.

She sipped from her wine and thought of the black cop who had been there with them as their lives had fallen apart. Clarence Simmons. She'd thought of him often over the years, giving him an almost mythic status. Knowing that she would be seeing him soon made her feel like she was taking a surreal step out of real life and into a place where dreams and nightmares never truly let go of you.

CHAPTER TWENTY EIGHT

As the afternoon progressed, two things happened. First, Chloe and Danielle somehow made it through three episodes of *House of Cards*. Second, the news crews seemed to have scattered away outside. As night fell, they seemed to be almost like pesky insects, flying off in search of whatever the next source of light might be.

They turned the TV off around nine. Chloe went through some of the still-unpacked boxes and found a spare toothbrush and pajamas for Danielle. Danielle refused the pajamas, selecting instead one of Chloe's basic black running tank tops. She was asleep by 9:45, crashing hard in the guest bedroom on a mattress that had not yet been placed on the bedframe, which was still disassembled and pushed against the wall. It made Chloe realize that given Steven's departure from her life, this house may never be fully unpacked. She wasn't sure she'd be able to afford it.

Chloe's head was too filled with ideas and worries to even think about sleep. She enjoyed a glass of wine all alone, sitting at the dining room table. She thought about maybe going back through the case files one more time but saw no sense in it. Until Alan Short was apprehended, there would likely be no forward progress on the case.

By the time she had finished her glass of wine, she realized that she and Danielle had polished off an entire bottle. She wasn't nearly drunk but was moderately lightheaded. Maybe she'd be able to get to sleep after all.

She made her way through the house, going through a routine that she supposed wasn't old enough to be a routine yet; she and Steven had only been here for a week now. The routine consisted of locking the doors—the front, the back, and the side door that led to the patio. Because of the remaining news crews outside (they were down to just two now), she also made a point to close all of the blinds as well.

As she made her way into the kitchen and to the back door that led to the back porch, she reached for the cord on the blinds to close them. Her hand paused before she could grab them.

There was something on the porch. It was a small picnic basket.

139

She thought for a moment, wondering if she should collect it. Was it perhaps some sort of peace offering from a reporter who had a change of heart? Or maybe they were from one of the police crews who had been standing guard outside all day.

No, she thought. *The cops would have let us know they were bringing it. And a reporter wouldn't risk coming all the way across the yard while the police were stationed at the sidewalk.*

Then what was in the basket? And who had put it there?

Going against her better judgment, Chloe quickly opened the back door. She snatched up the basket, took a quick look around to make sure there was no one waiting to ambush her on the porch, and then quickly stepped back inside. She locked the doors, closed the blinds, and set the picnic basket on the counter.

No sense in waiting or trying to talk myself out of it, she thought.

Holding her breath, she threw open the snap-case lid of the picnic basket.

There were a dozen or so cookies inside. Chocolate chip. From the look and the smell, they looked to have been made from scratch rather recently.

Her first thought was that someone was trying to poison them. But that was both stupid and almost fantastical. She stared at the cookies for a moment as if they might present some sort of a riddle. That's when she saw the corner of a piece of paper sticking out from beneath the parchment paper that held the cookies.

She grabbed the corner of the paper and pulled it out. It wasn't paper, not really. It was an envelope. An envelope with a golden sticker seal, just like the ones that had been delivered to Danielle's apartment.

She opened it slowly, as if she thought the contents of the envelope might actually be able to harm her. She made certain to only touch the very corners of the envelope and the flap. Of course, there was nothing inside but a letter. Still, the letter itself spoke volumes despite its short length.

IT'S NOT OVER.

She stared at the letter for a moment, and the envelope. She had intentionally only touched it by the corners. She was aware that the other letters had not held any fingerprints, but she wanted to check this one as well. She ventured into her bedroom and took her old evidence kit out—the very same one she had used for evidence labs during her first few years at the academy.

She quickly set up a little station on her kitchen counter, dusting for prints. As she had suspected, there were none. She then did the same to the basket and even the parchment paper that held the cookies. But there was nothing.

She stood there and looked at the unexpected delivery for a very long time. She considered waking Danielle but decided against it. With everything she had been through the last few days, this was the last thing she needed to deal with.

IT'S NOT OVER.

That's for damned sure, Chloe thought. Someone had managed to sneak into her backyard and leave this on her porch. Someone had trespassed on her property, had come within about two feet of her back door during one of the most stressful times of her life and were basically taunting her with this note.

No, she thought with some anger. *No, this isn't over by a long shot.*

CHAPTER TWENTY NINE

Even after several hours of sleep, Chloe decided not to tell Danielle about the basket of cookies and the letter. She'd disposed of the basket and cookies in the outside trashcan before retiring to bed, keeping only the letter. She read it once more as she woke up at six o'clock the following morning and then put it in the drawer of her bedside table.

When she went out to put the coffee on, she was not at all surprised to find that Danielle was apparently still asleep. As the coffee started to percolate, Chloe peeked into the guest bedroom and found her sister lightly snoring. *Good,* Chloe thought. *She needs her rest after all she's been through.*

Chloe picked at a small breakfast—a bowl of cereal and a banana—before finally getting dressed for the day. She thought she'd be more excited about potentially meeting with Clarence Simmons but she found that she was actually quite scared.

It's because you're digging up the past, she told herself. *And is that really any different than digging up a grave?* She thought of herself poised over her mother's grave with a shovel and something about the image nearly brought tears to her eyes.

She poured herself a thermos of coffee and then grabbed a Post-it from the kitchen bar. She scrawled a note on it for Danielle: *Gone to see Simmons. Will call when I'm on the way back. Make yourself at home and DO NOT LEAVE THE HOUSE.*

She headed outside and hurried to her car. There was only one news van and no one from it came rushing after her. She also saw the single police car parked adjacent to the news van. The officer watched her go to her car and even gave her a little wave. Chloe waved back, glad to see that the media circus had died down but, deep down in her guts, getting the feeling that this story was far from being over.

***

She made the drive from Pinecrest, Maryland, to Trenton, New Jersey, in just over two hours, speeding a bit most of the way. She pulled up in front of the Simmons residence at 9:42. She had not called in advance, not wanting to give him the opportunity to decline to speak with her. She had to hope that his retirement kept him at home, that he was more prone to kicking around the house than getting out and traveling.

Her hope was confirmed when she saw that the adjoining garage to the house was open. She saw a slightly overweight man petering around in the garage. He carried a screwdriver in his left hand and was studying a microwave oven that was sitting on a wooden table.

Chloe approached quietly but without stealth, not wanting to appear as if she was sneaking up on him. When it was clear that he had not yet heard her when she had closed in to just a few feet, she made her presence known.

"Mr. Simmons?"

He turned around to face her and it was like looking back into the past. The kind face that had remained with her and Danielle on that morning was very much the same. He now had a thin beard patched with gray and he had shaved his head at some point. But it was unmistakably him.

"That's me," he said. "But who's asking."

"I doubt you'd remember me," she said. "But we met briefly about seventeen years ago. My name is Chloe Fine."

His face went slack, though the start of a smile touched the corner of his mouth. He was in such shock that his fingers also went loose; the screwdriver fell from his grasp and clattered to the floor.

"Yeah, I remember," he said. "Good God, has it really been seventeen years?"

"It has," she said. "I was wondering if you wouldn't mind having a word with me."

Simmons still looked baffled but he nodded. "Yeah. Just trying to fix this microwave. Went on the fritz while I was heating up some sausage this morning." He scratched at his head and picked the screwdriver back up. "I assume this might be about what happened to your parents?"

"Yeah," she said. "And if it makes it any more pressing for you," she said, reaching into her pocket for her ID, "I'm interning at the FBI right now. On the way to becoming an agent."

He nodded as if he understood perfectly. "Lots of people that experience the sort of thing you did end up going into that line of work. My dad was shot and killed and then hung from a lamp post in North Carolina when I was seven years old. I knew by the time I was twelve that I wanted to be a policeman."

"So," she said, unsure how to handle his last comment. "Pinecrest didn't cut it for you after retirement?"

"No. My wife passed ten years ago and the rest of my family lives here in Jersey. Two sons and five grandkids."

"That sounds nice," she said.

"Yeah, it is," he said. "Anyway…what can I do for you, Ms. Fine?"

"Well, how well do you recall the case with my parents?"

"Clearly enough, I suppose. I remember that your father was just sort of sluggish when we took him in. Not much arguing and he didn't put up a fight. He went willingly. If you don't mind my saying so, it seemed like he had accepted what he had done and wanted to move on from it as quickly as possible."

"So there's no doubt in your mind that he did it?"

Simmons didn't answer right away. He tapped the screwdriver against the side of the microwave as he processed a few things.

"I never say there is no doubt," he said. "But from what I can remember, it was pretty clear that he was guilty. I'm sorry if that's not what you're wanting to hear but that's how I remember it. Now that you're older there are some aspects to the case you might want to know…maybe small things that were kept from you as a child. Are you okay hearing them?"

"Yes," she said, although she wasn't sure if this was true or not.

"Well, he was pretty much drunk when we took him in. Not wasted or hammered or anything, but he'd had a few. And keep in mind this was earlier in the day. I don't remember the time but it was well before lunch. Aside from you and your sister, he was the only one there and he *did* have motive after all."

"Motive?" Chloe asked, almost offended. "What kind of motive?"

Simmons looked uncomfortable, though he now discarded the screwdriver. The course of the conversation had clearly distracted him. He, too, was having to go back into his past to do some digging. Chloe knew all too well how unpleasant that could be.

"When we checked up on any alibis—none of which he really pushed too hard, mind you—we found that he had probably been sleeping with other women. There was no hard, concrete evidence of this, but the writing was right there on the wall. When we asked him if this was the case, he didn't deny it but he also never gave names."

"Did you ever have any names? Women you were pretty sure he was seeing?"

"I don't remember. I'm sure if you pulled the files, some names might be there. But good luck finding them. Seventeen years ago for a case that appeared to be a slam dunk from the get-go..."

"So the theory was that he killed my mother in the hopes of freeing himself so he could be with one of these other women?"

"I believe so, yes."

"And you are certain he was guilty?" she asked again.

"Sitting there with you two girls on those porch steps, I wanted him to be innocent. Right up until he basically admitted to seeing women on the side, I hoped for that. But...I'm sorry, Ms. Fine. Everything pointed to him being guilty."

"Was there ever any question that maybe someone else was there with him when it happened?"

"You mean did he act alone? Yeah, pretty sure of it. I mean...based on what I remember. It *has* been seventeen years, after all. Forgive me for asking, but is there any specific reason for asking so long after it happened?"

Chloe was slightly surprised. "Have you not seen the news in the last few days?"

"Nope," Simmons said. "I don't think I've watched a single minute of news coverage ever since Sandy Hook happened. Not for elections, not for lotto numbers, nothing."

Chloe thought about divulging everything to him but didn't see the point. Like just about everyone else familiar with her father's case, Simmons thought he had been guilty. And she doubted there would be much to change his mind seventeen years removed outside of solid evidence—and there was none of that.

"Well, thanks for your time," Chloe said. She was a bit frustrated that her two-hour drive had culminated in a conversation that had lasted less than fifteen minutes.

"I take it I didn't tell you what you were hoping to hear?"

"I don't know *what* I was hoping to hear," Chloe admitted.

He smiled at her and pointed toward the house. "Why don't you come inside and get a glass of tea or lemonade or something. Maybe we can go over the case in detail...maybe figure out how to get you the names of those women that might have known your father."

She nearly took him up on it. But then she thought about Danielle, sitting alone in her house with news crews outside, and knew she couldn't.

"Thanks for the invite, but I really need to get going."

Simmons nodded, as if he had expected as much. "Well, I hope you find whatever it is you're looking for."

You and me both, she thought as she headed back to her car.

She felt a bit like a spoiled brat, but hearing tales of how her father was sleeping around on her deceased mother was not how she wanted to spend her morning. And with that thought in her head, she headed back for Pinecrest with more questions than answers.

CHAPTER THIRTY

Chloe was a little over halfway home when she received a call from Greene. For a moment she worried that it would be about Danielle—that she had gone rogue and left her house, perhaps even trying to leave town. Or maybe the Alan Short thing had fallen through and all signs were pointing back to Danielle again.

She answered the call before these speculations could get the better of her. "Good news?" she asked hopefully.

"Depends on how you look at it," Greene said. "Pinecrest PD had a few officers go by the residence of Alan Short. He wasn't home. Turns out he hasn't been to work in the past two days, either."

"That would be *bad* news, then," Chloe said. "He's apparently making a run for it."

"That's true. But some might also see it as a sign of guilt—of a sign of needing to get away from something. What about you? Did you meet with your retired cop?" Chloe had informed Greene of her mission before leaving that morning.

"I did. But I don't think it really did much. In an odd way, I guess it *did* help to have some closure from that morning. Simmons seemed absolutely sure my dad was guilty. Said there were a few affairs around town that basically proved it."

"Well, at least you tried, right?"

"Right. Thanks for the update. You sure there's nothing I can do?"

"You can get back home to your sister as quick as you can. Once news gets out that there is a search for a second suspect, the reporters might come out of the woodwork for Danielle again, wanting to know how it feels to be free. Consider this your first lesson in media relations: they won't stop until after the story is done, run into the ground, and retread about one hundred times."

"Thanks for the tip," Chloe said.

Though honestly, if a few more irritating reporters was going to be the worst of what she'd have to put up with before this was all over, she thought that might be okay with her.

But then her thoughts went back to the basket of cookies and the note.

147

IT'S NOT OVER.

And for reasons she could not explain, that damned note was starting to seem like some dark prophecy.

***

After she got back home, Chloe was relieved to find that Danielle had indeed stayed put. Her rebellious side seemed to even have the most foundational laws of safety and good sense down. When she got home, Chloe found Danielle looking around on the Internet. The current article she had up was telling what sort of man Martin Shields was.

"I had no idea the asshole had two DUIs on his record," Danielle exclaimed. "No wonder he always looked tense and nervous whenever he got behind the wheel."

"Well, I suppose today is the day to learn new things about people we thought we knew," Chloe said.

"What do you mean? What did Simmons know?"

"Well, he stands by the ruling that dad was guilty. Said Dad confessed to the murder. Said he confessed to a lot more, too. Namely at least one affair. He was apparently seeing a few other women while he was married to Mom."

"Bullshit."

Chloe shrugged helplessly. "I'd like to think so. But Simmons had a straight head on his shoulders and he seemed so sure."

"Aren't there records and files for this kind of shit?" Danielle asked.

"Yes, but he said they'd take some digging to find. And if it comes to that, I think I'm prepared to do that digging. But I don't know that we'd really need to. I was thinking about something the whole ride back here. Let's say Dad *was* cheating. In a town like this, someone would know about it. Word gets around. And I think a good place to start would be with the book club. *Someone* there knew Mom or Dad, even if it *was* just Tammy Wyler."

"Oh yeah! She wouldn't shut up about the fucking book club at the block party! How did I miss that?"

"Don't feel bad. I almost did, too. The fight between Steven and Martin basically dwarfed anything else that happened that day."

"So you want to what? Join a book club?"

"Sure," Chloe said, already taking out her phone. "Why not?"

She typed in *Pinecrest Public Library* and then *book club*. She was directed to the Pinecrest Public Library website. There, she found the current book the club was reading (*Sharp Objects* by Gillian Flynn) and when the club typically met (Tuesdays and Thursdays, at six o'clock in the evening). She also found the phone number and extension for the woman who managed the book club, a lady by the name of Mary Elder.

She pressed the number on her screen and the phone placed the call. She listened to it ring in her ear until it was answered on the third ring.

"Pinecrest Public Library," a woman said.

"Yes, hi," Chloe said, doing her best to shrug off the nerves and exhaustion the last few days had set upon her. It was hard to sound cheerful, but she did her best. "I was wondering if there was any process for joining the book club. Any paperwork or anything?"

"No ma'am," the equally cheerful voice replied. "Just a contact form where we ask about reading preferences and things like that. Are you interested in joining? We meet on Tuesdays and Thursdays, so you'd be welcome to come to the meeting tonight. The club is about one hundred pages into the current book, but that's okay."

"You know, I think I might just do that," Chloe said. "Six o' clock, right?"

"That's right. Can I get your name so we can go ahead and be expecting you?"

Chloe gave her name and felt like she had tossed a grenade at the poor lady. "Chloe Fine."

"Oh, okay," Mary Elder said, clearly taken off guard. "We'll be happy to have you." There was something like sympathy in her voice. Chloe leaped at it like a fish to bait.

"I know, I know," she said. "Seems weird. And I don't want to cause any distraction at the club. I just need to get away from all of the drama, you know? And I heard someone in my neighborhood say that my mother used to be in a book club...maybe the same one, I don't know. I thought it might help."

"Oh, of course," Mary Elder said. "I remember your mother a bit, actually. And it would be lovely to have to join us. I'll put an extra seat out tonight."

Chloe smiled. She was a better actress than she'd thought. "I look forward to it," she said.

Chloe ended the call and found Danielle grinning at her. "Well, you're just a filthy little liar, aren't you?"

"Hey, I like to read."

"I do, too," Danielle said. "Can I tag along?"

149

"I don't think that would be the best idea. Even though the headlines have started to indicate that you might not be guilty, you know how this town is. You'd be shunned."

Danielle sighed and got to her feet. She went into the kitchen and popped the top off of another bottle of wine, regardless that it was only two in the afternoon.

"Well, if I'm staying here by myself again, you might need to go out and get more wine."

They shared a laugh—a sound that was alien to both of them. It seemed out of place in the quiet house with the remaining news crew and police car buzzing around outside. But it was the first time since she had returned to Pinecrest that Chloe thought things might turn out all right between them.

Of course, all they had to do now was completely clear Danielle's name.

CHAPTER THIRTY ONE

The Pinecrest Public Library was surprisingly large for the size of the town it accommodated. It was two stories tall, the bottom portion mostly dedicated to children's and middle grade books. When Chloe entered at 5:57 to join the book club, she was directed to the back of the bottom level by a series of signs adorned with arrows and the heading of BOOK CLUB.

She followed the signs to a cozy-looking conference room where several folding chairs had been set up in a semicircle. A small table was set up in the back with bottles of water and light snacks. A few women had already arrived, sitting in some of the chairs and in the midst of conversation. A woman who had been standing by the table in the back came up to her with a smile on her face.

"Hello there," this woman said. "I'm Mary Elder. I organize the book club."

"Oh, nice to meet you," Chloe said.

Mary Elder looked to be pushing sixty. If she had been here twenty years ago, the idea that she had interacted with her mother in the midst of this very book club was not too farfetched.

"I'm so glad you could join us. If you need a copy of the book, we have a few extras."

Chloe did not have the book, nor did she intend to start reading it. "Oh, that's okay. I have it at home and forgot to bring it. I'm about halfway through it."

"Great! Well, have a seat or help yourself to some snacks. We'll begin soon."

But Chloe barely heard the end of this comment. Instead, her attention was on the door. A familiar face walked through and when that face turned in Chloe's direction, it was filled with shock.

Ruthanne Carwile stood there, frozen for a moment, as if she had looked directly into the eyes of a ghost. She entered the room slowly, finally giving Chloe a little nod of recognition before taking a seat next to a group of three women.

Chloe ventured to the back table, giving the room and its participants some room to breathe—to operate the way it usually did when there wasn't a stranger around. She watched as small groups of friends joined together while Mary Elder took a seat at the end of the semicircle. By Mary taking her seat, it appeared that the other eleven women in the room took this to mean that it was time for the meeting to begin.

Chloe took a water and then found a seat. She took one across the semicircle from Ruthanne, wanting to keep an eye on her. The way Ruthanne had looked at her made her a little wary. There had been a split second where Chloe had seen pure disdain; it was clear that Ruthanne was not happy that Chloe was there.

"Before we get into the book tonight," Mary said, "I wanted to introduce our new member. And Chloe, this isn't calling you out...we do this to all new members. So everyone, please welcome a Pinecrest local who has just recently come back into town, Chloe Fine."

There were a few strange faces around the room. No one knew how to react to her presence. They'd obviously all seen the news headlines and, even if that were not the case, would likely all know about her history. She was the youngest person in the room, with the closest runner-up being about thirty or so, she guessed.

Mary seemed to sense the tension and did her best to tame it. But by the time two words had come out of her mouth, Chloe realized that the librarian was unintentionally helping her out.

"I remember when Chloe's mother used to be in this club," she said. "She was always so insightful and just a ton of fun to be around. Chloe, I'm very glad to have you join us and hope you can bring that same level of insight your mother did."

"I'll try my best," Chloe said. She then looked around the room and tried to put on her best sympathetic look—not quite saddened, but somewhere closer to reflective. "If you don't mind my asking, was anyone else in the room a member when Mom was here?"

She knew that if anyone in the room was sentimental, they'd speak up. She hated to play on people's emotions but she had to bet that recent news headlines would cause them to assume that she was here mainly to escape the drama of her sister and to perhaps find some old memories of her mother for peace.

As she expected, it worked.

Two women raised their hands, neither of whom was Ruthanne Carwile.

"I was part of the club when Gale was a member," one of the women said. "And Mary is right...she was so into reading. Always had some insights into the books that I could never even dream of.

And she sometimes brought this cheese dip she made herself. It was delicious."

"My goodness," the other woman said. "I nearly forgot about Gale Fine's cheese dip."

"You know," Mary said, "I believe she also volunteered a few hours a week to help tutor kids that had problems reading. I'd have to go back into the records to look into that, but I think—"

"She did," Ruthanne said. Her voice had very little cheer to it and when she spoke, she did not look at Chloe.

What the hell is her deal? Chloe wondered.

"I thought so," Mary said.

Silence filled the room again. That awkward tension fell upon them once more and this time, it caused Ruthanne to stand up. She looked around the room apologetically, only glancing in Chloe's direction for a split second.

"I'm sorry," she said. "Excuse me for a moment." Ruthanne then exited the semicircle, leaving her book behind, and quickly left the room.

"Forgive me for asking, dear," the older woman who had mentioned the cheese dip said. "How well do you remember her?" She nodded toward the door as she asked, indicating the question was regarding Ruthanne.

"A bit. I ran into her at a Lavender Hills block party and some things came back to me. She would hang out with Mom every now and then, I think. Danielle and I would watch cartoons in her living room. And I think she used to make us grilled cheeses for lunch some afternoons when she and Mom were hanging out."

"Ruthanne took it hard when your mother died," Mary said. "She stopped coming to the book club for about six months. It was odd because no one realized they were so close." Mary then paused and looked around the room. "Dear, I'm so sorry. I don't know how this became all about you and your mother. I feel like we sort of ambushed you there."

"No, no, not at all. I actually appreciate it. Actually, if you don't mind, I do have one more question I was hoping someone might be able to answer."

No one gave a nod yes, but no one shut it down, either. So Chloe asked her question.

"Near the end of Mom's life, was there anything she said or did to make someone think she might be scared or in trouble?"

It was clear that the question was too much for some in the room. A few people were flipping through their books, even studying the notes they had taken. Really, it was just Mary Elder and the woman Chloe now thought of as Cheese Dip Lady that looked engaged.

"No, not really," Mary said. She then looked to the door where Ruthanne had just made her exit. "I…well, I don't know that this would be the appropriate time or place to talk about these things."

"I understand," Chloe said, sensing her window of opportunity closing. "If I could—"

"There were rumors," Cheese Dip Lady said. "About your father. With all due respect, aren't you working for the FBI? I assume anything we have to say about him, you've probably already discovered on your own. That being said…yes, there were rumors. Rumors that your father was having an affair."

"Yes, I know those rumors."

Cheese Dip Lady then also looked toward the door. She said nothing but that gesture was more than enough to get her point across.

There were rumors that your father was having an affair with Ruthanne Carwile.

It was then Chloe's turn to stand up and excuse herself. She looked to Mary Elder with sincere apology in her eyes. Any idea that she had come here tonight to actually enjoy a book club had been dashed.

"I'm so sorry," she said. "I think I need to be excused, too."

"Chloe," Mary said. "Maybe wait awhile."

Oh, I plan to, she thought as she exited the semicircle. As she headed for the door, a thought occurred to her—one that was so simple and outrageous at the same time that it might just lead somewhere.

Before leaving, she walked behind the semicircle to the place where Ruthanne had been sitting. Chloe picked up the copy of *Sharp Objects* Ruthanne had left behind. Her eyes briefly studied the small slip of paper that was barely sticking out between the pages.

"I'll make sure she gets this," Chloe said.

Very few of the women met her gaze and those who did looked worried and very awkward. With that, Chloe took her leave and rushed out to her car. She didn't even bother looking for any signs of Ruthanne in the parking lot. She got behind the wheel of her car and opened up the book. In the waning light of the afternoon, she flipped through the pages, working on a hunch.

She found what she was looking for at the very back of the book. It was a single sheet of notebook paper with a few notes about the book scrawled across it. The print was pretty and quite legible.

With her heart beating a little faster, Chloe set the book in the passenger seat and started the car. She headed for work, feeling confident she'd have plenty of space to work in the practice lab at this hour.

Leaving the library, she called Greene. She felt that at this stage, with such a huge hunch taking form, she might need a bit more experience on her side. Greene answered right away, sounding hopeful but also a little distant.

"Have a productive day?" he asked.

"I think maybe I did," she said. "Are you available right now?"

"Well, I just finished dinner with the family. What do you need?"

"Is there any way you can meet me down at the lab sometime soon? I have something I think might be worth looking into."

"Give me an hour. And please don't take this the wrong way, but distance yourself from the case. Pretend your sister isn't involved. Would it still be worth looking into?"

Chloe was thinking about the basket of cookies that had been delivered to her porch, hiding a very simple note inside.

A note with very precise penmanship.

"Absolutely," she answered.

CHAPTER THIRTY TWO

When Chloe arrived at the lab, Greene was not there yet. The hour he'd requested still had another fifteen minutes attached to it. Still, Chloe found a workspace at the lab (there was only one other intern working in the entire lab, doing something with an old glove) and set up. She took Ruthanne Carwile's notes of out of the copy of *Sharp Objects* and set it out beside the envelope that contained the letter that had come with the box of cookies.

As Chloe took the letter out of the envelope, she felt like she was stepping through a door—and that door might close behind her and trap her in this new place. And that was fine with her. Because that new place was a world where her studying of handwriting analysis and her subsequent excelling at it was no longer something she did for practice; she was putting it to use now and it could very well free Danielle for good.

She scanned in both handwriting examples, first the letter and then the notes. She then uploaded them to the cloud and powered up her iPad. She opened up a side-by-side comparison of the samples and within five seconds was pretty sure she had a match. Of course, as an intern who had already been given a rather long leash, she needed Green to confirm it.

While she waited, she tried to imagine why Ruthanne Carwile would be sending Danielle threatening letters. Such an act might make sense if it was someone younger, someone like Kathleen Saunders who had gone to high school with them. But Ruthanne was much older, pushing fifty—the age their mother would have been if she were still alive.

So maybe there's something to that, she thought. *Ruthanne knew my mother well enough to have her over for drinks while Danielle and I watched cartoons in her living room. With that sort of familiarity, how well did she know Dad?*

The thought raced across her mind that perhaps it had indeed been Ruthanne that her father had been having an affair with. It would explain why Ruthanne had so quickly exited the book club when the conversation turned to Chloe's parents.

She tried to think of how to find out if there was any merit to this aside from contacting Ruthanne personally. She was about to call Danielle with this theory—perhaps asking if she'd ever had any odd moments with Ruthanne either in their youth or after she came back to Pinecrest—when Agent Greene stepped into the lab.

"So where are we at?" he asked, taking a seat beside her at the exam table.

She quickly ran through the course of her day, filling him in on her nearly fruitless conversation with Clarence Simmons and ending with finding the notes in Ruthanne's copy of *Sharp Objects*. She then told him about finding the basket of cookies with the hidden note on her back porch last night.

"They must have been staking the place hard," Greene said, a bit disappointed. "They'd have to have been watching the shift changes with the officers outside of your house in order to get into your backyard. I'll have to take that up with the Pinecrest PD. That's inexcusable."

"It is, but that's okay for now. Look…I scanned in Ruthanne Carwile's notes and placed them alongside a scan from the letter that came last night."

She showed him her iPad screen where the two scans still sat side by side. "In my estimation," she said, "there are at least four similarities to the handwriting that make this a match. But I think the most telling one can be found on the way she ends her unconnected Rs."

She then zoomed in to the R in the letter: *IT'S NOT OVER.*

It was capitalized, as was the heading on the notes from the book that read: *GROWTH VS. FEAR.*

She caught Greene smiling a bit as he gave her a nod. "And what would you say the second most striking resemblance is?" he asked, quizzing her.

Even in the excitement of a moment such as this, she did not mind him quizzing her. It kept her focused and made her distance herself from the personal nature of the case.

"I'd say either the slanted elongated shape of her capital O or the straight, unbent shape of her apostrophe." She pointed to the apostrophe on *IT'S* from the letter and several apostrophes within the notes.

"I'm happy to say," Greene said, "that while it would still be subject to scrutiny, this is more than enough to pursue Ruthanne Carwile as the person who has been delivering the notes to your sister. But I'm afraid it will do basically nothing in furthering the case for Danielle's innocence. Still…a great find."

"So how quickly can we move on this?" she asked.

"Always so eager," Greene said with a chuckle. "I'll call Johnson and fill him in on this detail. The fact that this most recent letter was sent while your sister was the subject of a murder investigation makes it extremely bad for Ms. Carwile. And while I call, you drive."

"Drive where?"

"To wherever this woman lives. Your neighborhood, right? Based on this handwriting analysis, we've got enough to bring her in for questioning at the very least. If we wanted to *really* push, we could charge her with interfering in a federal murder investigation. Seriously, Fine…this is some great work."

Chloe took the compliment but tucked it away for later. In her mind's eye, she saw her house and then the streets that connected all of Lavender Hills. Danielle would be at her house, alone and waiting for an update. Meanwhile, one street over and half a block down, Ruthanne Carwile was sitting in her own home, maybe pondering the next threatening letter she'd write for Danielle.

It was frightening in a way she could not explain. And it also pissed her off.

"Yeah," she said, shutting down her iPad and getting to her feet. "Let's go get her."

CHAPTER THIRTY THREE

Chloe looked at Ruthanne through the one-way glass. The woman looked like a dog that had been scolded, tossed into a cage, and wasn't sure who to trust. There was a rather humane moment where Chloe felt bad for her. It was clear that Ruthanne Carwile had never expected to spend a second of her privileged life in an interrogation room. She was looking around the room as if she had stepped through a doorway into another world.

There were two men in the room with her—a cop who stood by the door with his arms folded over his chest, and a Pinecrest detective named Peterson. Their presence seemed to jolt her. It had been Chloe and Greene who had come to her house, after all. She had likely been expecting to see a familiar face while she was being questioned.

"Will I get to speak with her?" Chloe asked.

"Not unless it's absolutely necessary," Greene said. "Think about it...she'd try to use the fact that she knew your mother against you. She may even get defensive enough to try making you feel small—making you feel like that little girl that used to sit on her living room floor watching TV."

Chloe nodded. She had figured as much. She was nervous but not as much as she thought she'd be. She had interrogated two suspects before, as part of her training. To this day, she was pretty sure one of them had been fake, just a stand-in for the purpose of her coursework. So if she *did* get to speak with her, she felt confident that she could be effective.

She and Green watched as Peterson did a fine job with his own interrogation. It wasn't in-your-face or hostile but there was a sense of urgency to every word that came out of his mouth.

He slid a printout of the scans Chloe had created across the table to her. Ruthanne looked at them and revealed that she had perhaps the world's worst poker face.

"We know for a fact that one of these is yours," Peterson said. "And after scanning them and placing them side by side, it looks like they're *both* yours. Would you like to take a guess as to which is which?"

Ruthanne pointed to the paper, tapping the right side. "These are my notes from my book club. They were in my book."

"Yes, that's right," Peterson said. "And what about this other one? What about this one little sentence? *It's not over.* What's that mean?"

Ruthanne shook her head. "I don't know. That's not from my notes."

"Oh, I know that," Peterson said. "See, this note was delivered to Danielle Fine last night, while she was staying with her sister. And the reason we're asking you about it is because even you can surely see how similar the penmanship is."

"I see that, yes. But I did not write that."

Peterson nodded and then gave her another sheet of paper. It was murky through the glass but Peterson saw that it was a picture of Martin Shields. "Does this man look familiar to you?" Peterson asked.

Ruthanne nodded and said: "Yes. He was at the block party in Lavender Hills last weekend. He got into a fight with Chloe Fine's fiancé."

"And did you know that he turned up dead just several days later?"

"I did know that. One of my friends heard about it and told me."

"Had you ever spoken with or seen Mr. Shields at any time before the block party?" Peterson asked.

"No, sir."

Chloe was studying her closely. Watching Ruthanne's face was like a case study of recognizing facial tics. When she told the truth—when she denied something and actually *meant* it—the relief was evident on her face. But when she lied, her responses were quick and her face would tense up as if she had smelled something unpleasant.

"And did you speak with him during the block party?"

"I don't think so. And if I did, it was nothing more than a *hello* or a *nice to meet you.*"

Peterson leaned back in his chair and nodded sympathetically. Chloe thought he was very good at what he did. He was making it seem as if he thought it was a little silly that they had pulled this poor innocent woman out of her home to answer such dumb questions.

"Now, I understand that you knew Chloe Fine and her sister back when they were kids...that you and their mother were friends."

"We were for a while, yes. Not very close, but we'd enjoy a drink together every now and then."

"The girls would sometimes watch cartoons in your living room while you and their mother hung out on the porch, correct?"

"Correct," Ruthanne said. The expression on her face made it clear that she was not comfortable with where the conversation was headed.

"Do you recall what sort of conversations you had with her?"

Ruthanne squirmed a bit in her chair and took a moment to gather her answer. "Not really. Probably just work stuff. Complaining about work, marriages, and so on."

"Was Mrs. Fine not happy in her marriage?"

Ruthanne actually cringed at the question. "There were times when she wasn't."

"And were you there for her during those times? Did she come to your house to seek some of that talking time on the porch?"

"No."

"Do you know why not?"

"I'm sorry," Ruthanne said. "What does this have to do with anything?"

It was Peterson who bristled this time, not liking that he had been interrupted. He again pushed the handwriting analysis over to her. "Well, I'm trying to figure out why someone would send such mean letters to Danielle Fine. You see...this letter is not the first. And what that means is that we have at least five more letters that we can scan and compare to your book club notes. And I have to tell you, Ms. Carwile...based on just this one comparison right here, I think we're going to find quite a lot."

"I didn't write this note," she said. But she was close to tears and could no longer look at the paper.

"Are you sure?" Peterson asked. "Because here's the deal...whoever dropped this note off on Chloe Fine's back porch did so while Danielle was part of a murder investigation. That makes this more than just a threatening note. It makes it interference in a federal case. And that's a hefty fine...maybe even some jail time. So I want this cleared up as soon as possible. If whoever wrote this can fess up now and issue an apology to Danielle Fine, I think the matter can be settled without any fuss. So let me ask you again before this gets out of hand...did you write this note and the others that came before it?"

Ruthanne answered in a sob that seemed to surprise her as it came out of her throat. She slapped the two papers Peterson had showed her off of the table.

"Yes," she said. "I sent the notes."

Peterson gave her a moment before he pressed on. "Can you tell me why?"

She shook her head. "It was a bitch thing to do. I never liked that girl. And her being in Pinecrest, coming back after failing elsewhere, it reminded me..."

Something then seemed to snap into place for Ruthanne. She sat up and looked to the glass. "Is Chloe back there?" she asked Peterson. "Chloe, I'm sorry. And you can tell Danielle, too. I'm sorry about the notes. It was stupid and immature..."

"Okay, so now please try to follow me," Peterson said. "You sent Danielle those letters for what you say are stupid reasons. Jealousy, maybe? Or maybe you just straight up don't like her. Honestly, I don't care. And now that you've admitted it, it's not an issue. However...part of my job is to try to find threads in things. And if you knew Chloe and Danielle Fine's mother—Gale Fine— and sent these messages to Danielle seventeen years later, it makes me wonder why.

"You see, we've now discovered that it's a well-trod theory that Aiden Fine was having at least one affair. And while no one ever came forward with one, someone that maybe spent routine time with his wife, learning about him and his schedule..."

"Absolutely not," Ruthanne said. She said it quickly but with a bit of shock, but still Chloe wasn't sure she was telling the truth.

"Okay, I believe you," he said, though Chloe wasn't sure he did. "Do you happen to remember where you were on the day Gale Fine was killed?"

"I was at home. I remember getting the call, but I don't remember who it was. I heard that she had been killed, that he was on his way to prison, and the girls were sent off to their grandparents."

"Let me ask you *this,* then," Peterson said. "All of this happened in Pinecrest. Their deaths, the girls being carted off to the grandparents'...and your friendship with their mother. How long have you lived in Pinecrest?"

"I've been here for years," she said. "I moved from Boston to Pinecrest with my first husband. When we divorced, I nearly moved to Baltimore. But I met a man during my hunt for a house and he lived in Pinecrest. We got married and bought a house in Pinecrest so I stayed put."

"But you and your husband…your second husband, that is, are no longer together, correct?"

"Right. We divorced last year. He moved to Texas and left me the house."

"Is that when you started sending the notes to Danielle Fine?"

Ruthanne shook her head. "This was about six months ago when I started doing that."

"And you still don't have a good reason?"

"No."

She's lying, Chloe thought.

On the other side of the glass, Peterson got up and looked down at her. "Let me check on a few things," he said. "I think I can get you away from all of this with just a slap on the wrist in terms of the letters. Hang tight, okay? I'll have you out of here as soon as I can."

The relief in her face was so clear that it was jarring. *She's hiding something,* Chloe thought.

Peterson left the interrogation room and came into the little observation area. He joined Chloe and Greene, staring at Ruthanne through the glass.

"So," he said. "She's lying her ass off. I just can't tell about what."

"She knows more than she's letting on," Chloe said.

"She does," Peterson said.

"It also makes me think that maybe she knew your father better than she's letting on," Green said. "That or your grandparents."

"What if she really knows what happened to my mother?" Chloe asked. "She could have the answers to the whole thing…"

Greene made a startled motion as his cell phone buzzed inside of his pocket. He took it out and read the text message that had just come through.

"Maybe she does," Greene said. "We can start looking for ourselves if you want. I just got a notice that we've got a search warrant for her house approved."

Chloe looked at the harmless-looking woman on the other side of the glass. She barely remembered the woman from her childhood, but she *could* remember sitting in front of her TV with Danielle.

Had Ruthanne been keeping secrets even then?

Chloe felt a little sneer come to her face as she started for the door. Green quickly thanked Peterson for his hard work and then followed her out. Chloe wasn't sure but she thought he seemed as if he was now just as anxious to get to the bottom of it all as she was.

CHAPTER THIRTY FOUR

They walked up Ruthanne's porch steps under the cover of night as the late summer evening chewed through its last bit of evening light. It glowed like an angry strip of red along the horizon. Chloe watched as Greene expertly picked both the key lock and the dead bolt. It took him less than twenty seconds and then they were stepping inside Ruthanne's house.

The place was meticulously cleaned and smelled like a mixture of lemon and vanilla. It was one of the smaller houses on the street but the inside was still quite beautiful. The front door opened into a small foyer with high ceilings. This took them into an alcove where a right-hand turn would take them into the kitchen and a left-hand turn would lead into the living room.

Chloe stayed with Greene, not quite sure what they were looking for just yet. *If she knows the truth about Mom, what form would that truth take? If it's something more than just firsthand knowledge, what else would she have?*

"Can you think of anything your mother might have given this woman while they were friends?" Greene asked.

"No. I really barely even remember her at all."

"So based on what we know and what we *anticipate,* what do you think we should be looking for?"

"If we want immediate answers, I don't know," she said. "If we can find a laptop, I think we need to take it. Maybe there are documents or receipts or…I don't know. Something. Or maybe we could get into her emails. Her phone would be the best bet, but she had that on her at the station."

"I'm going to give you ten minutes to look the place over," Greene said. With that, he took out his phone and started scrolling through his contacts. "In the meantime, I'm going to call Peterson and see what they can do to get her phone from her. We'd basically have to charge her with something at that point, though. And at this stage, that will be tough."

Chloe again found herself appreciating the lengths Greene was going to allow her to learn unhindered. But at the same time, she was very aware of each and every step she made through Ruthanne's house as she started her search. She scanned the living room and did see a laptop sitting on the edge of a walnut coffee table. She figured it was worth a try, so she opened it up but was presented with a password screen. Frowning, Chloe left it and headed further into the living room.

She came to a small hallway that contained only a coat closet, a bathroom, and the staircase to the second floor. The stairway brought her to another hallway. This one contained another bathroom and two bedrooms. The first bedroom was rather small and was filled with boxes. Chloe checked the boxes and found an assortment of things that made her wonder if Ruthanne had considered moving away from Pinecrest recently. There were books, a spare coffeemaker, unopened packs of toilet paper, tampons, Q-tips, and other toiletries. There were also several boxes of clothes that had been packed up.

Chloe left this makeshift storage room and walked into the other bedroom. This was the master, as immaculately cleaned as the rest of the house. A queen-sized bed sat in the center of the room, against the far wall. Pushed into the right corner of the room was a small desk. An iPad and a few books sat on the top of it. Off to the side, there was a small organization cube, the type that helped to sort letters, paper, correspondence, and so forth.

Chloe found the exact same kind of envelopes and little golden seals that had been used to deliver the notes to Danielle. She thumbed through them, wondering if maybe she pre-wrote the letters. But all she found were blank pages.

A small ornate filing cabinet sat beneath the desk. It was the kind of thing that looked like it was more for decoration than serving an actual purpose, made of wicker and frilly bronze knobs. It was no larger than two feet high, fitting perfectly beneath the desk. Chloe dropped to her knees and pulled out the first of the two drawers. There were a few scattered pictures, some showing Ruthanne with a man whom Chloe assumed was one of her husbands. Judging by the clothes, she supposed they were no older than ten years old.

In the back of the drawer, she found a battered-looking photo album, the collectible kind that only held one or two a page.

She opened it up and nearly dropped it.

There was a picture of her parents in the first sleeve. Her mother was grinning widely while her father gave her a kiss on the cheek. With trembling fingers, Chloe turned the page. This time the picture was just her father. He was looking away from the camera, his gaze following that of a young girl...

That's either me or Danielle, she thought. She'd seen enough of their childhood pictures to recognize the frizzy blonde hair.

"What the hell?" she said.

She kept turning and saw three more pictures of her family. Her mother was only in one more of them. The focal point of the pictures was undoubtedly her father.

She turned yet another page and it was like jumping forward in time. She saw her father again, but he was older. His hair was graying and his eyes looked tired. More than that, this one appeared to be a selfie. There was a concrete wall behind him, scarred and cracked, likely the inside of a cell or some sort of resource room at his prison.

He's got to be at least forty in this picture, Chloe thought. *Oh my God...this is recent.* Very *recent, maybe.*

There were two more recent pictures of her father. Each one was more jarring than the one before it. Chloe hated to admit it, but she had the intense urge to cry. Yes, she and Danielle had willingly made the decision to just pretend he no longer existed—but that had been *after* he had started to ignore them. To see him in the present, sending pictures of himself to someone they barely knew...it felt obscene.

She came to the end of the album and instantly went to the bottom drawer. The only thing in it was an old cardboard keepsake box. It had a flimsy little decorative latch keeping it closed. She broke it off in her hurry to open the box.

Inside, she found several folded sheets of paper. But sitting on top of them all was a phone. It was an iPhone, about two models behind the most recent. Taking a chance, she tried to power it on. She waited until the Apple logo came on, the loading bar starting to fill beneath it.

While she waited, she took one of the folded pieces of paper at random. She unfolded it and found a right-leaning script that had made up a letter that occupied about half a page. She barely even scanned the letter itself. She went straight to the salutation.

A little cry of sadness rose out of her throat when she saw her father's name.

* * *

"Agent Greene!"

She called his name, not giving a damn that her voice was thick with emotion and that she was on the verge of crying.

167

"Coming!" he said. He sounded concerned, as did his footfalls as she listened to them coming up the stairs.

While she waited for him, she looked at another of the letters. Without counting, she supposed there were at least twenty in all. She scanned this letter a little more closely before coming to her father's name again. Some of the words she saw included: *never loved her, soulmate, anything for you, be together again soon* and *deepest love.*

She wanted to tear the letter to shreds. She might have done just that if Greene had not come into the room in that moment.

"What is it?" he asked, his hand hovering over his sidearm. She supposed her voice *had* been rather alarming.

"She *was* having an affair with him. It's here…in these letters. I don't know how far it goes back, but some of this paper looks old and worn. And then there's this," she said, sliding the photo album his way. "There are pictures of our family in here and…and recent pictures of my dad."

"What about this?" Greene asked, picking up the old iPhone.

"I don't know yet."

The phone had fully booted up, allowing Greene to look it over. He went to Pictures and found the gallery empty. He then checked for texts but found not a single one. But when he checked the call history, he found pay dirt. He showed the screen to Chloe. She observed the six listings, noting that they were all made to the same number.

"You recognize this number?" Greene asked.

"No. But they're all made on the same day…on Tuesday of this week."

"The day Martin Shields was killed," Greene said, finishing her thought for her.

Without another word, Greene instantly pulled out his phone and made a call. Chloe only half listened as she picked up another letter and read it. This time, she read it word for word.

Ruthie,

It was good seeing you last week, even it if was *through the dirty glass. I can't tell you how much it means to me that you still come all the way out here to see me. But just think…another year or two and there will be no more waiting. No more long trips. I'll be with you all the time.*

I think of you all the time. It makes the nights longer, but that's okay. You're the only reason I have to even look forward to getting

out. Two years...two measly years. You can wait that long for me,
right? I hope so.

Write me back when you can. And if it's not asking too much,
could you send another of your "special" pictures? Maybe
something with black lace this time?

Yours,
Aiden

There was too much in the letter to process. For starters...two
years. What about two years? She was pretty sure she knew what it
meant but...*how?*

Greene had gotten off the phone. Distantly, Chloe was aware
that he had called someone at the bureau to trace down the owner of
the number they had found on the stow-away phone.

"Find something?" he asked.

She nodded and handed him the letter she had just read. "Can
you make a call and find out what my father's status is? I haven't
cared for so long...I just figured he'd rot in prison. Was that naïve
of me?"

"I don't know enough about the case to say for sure," Greene
said as he scanned through the letter. "Jesus, Chloe...this is rough.
I'm sorry you're uncovering all of this."

"I'm not," she said, meaning it. She was, however, finding it
very hard to imagine telling Danielle everything she had discovered
during the course of this day.

When Greene's phone rang, it startled them both. He looked at
the display and said, "They must have a name for that number
already."

He answered it and Chloe waited patiently, listening to only
Greene's side of the conversation.

"That was quick...yeah." A pause and then, very slowly,
Greene added: "Can you please repeat that?...Yeah, okay. Thanks."

He killed the call and looked gravely at Chloe. "Pick up those
letters and anything else you found. We're taking them to her as
proof. This thing just blew up on her."

"Why?" Chloe asked. "Greene...whose number is that in the
phone?"

He smiled, as if he couldn't believe their luck. "It appears that
Ruthanne Carwile has been using that old phone to call Alan
Short."

It took a full second for the name to register. Alan Short—the man who had somehow gotten some of his blood under Martin's fingernails.

"Holy shit," she said.

"It's enough for a conspiracy charge," Greene said. "And if we push hard enough, probably enough to free your sister."

Danielle, Chloe thought, again sickened by the fact that she was going to have to relay all of this information to her.

But first there was Ruthanne to deal with. And truth be told, Chloe couldn't wait to see the look on that bitch's face when she plopped these letters and pictures down in front of her.

CHAPTER THIRTY FIVE

Earlier, Chloe thought Ruthanne had looked like a scared dog inside the interrogation room. But now, as she was forced to watch things unfold from the other side of the glass again, it was *Chloe* who felt like a dog. Only she imagined this might be what a dog felt like when it was chained to a post and *really* wanted to get after the maimed rabbit at the edge of the yard, wanting to tear its throat out.

It was made worse by the fact that she was in the observation room alone. Greene had joined Peterson in the interrogation room. As she watched, both men stood on the opposite side of the table from Ruthanne. Greene held a manila envelope under his arm. Ruthanne had noticed it and couldn't seem to take her eyes away from it.

Peterson wasted no time with pleasantries this time. He leaned over the table, closing the space between them significantly.

"I'm going to ask you this last time…and I want you to think long and hard about your answer," he said. "Were you at any point in the last twenty years or so involved in an affair with Aiden Fine?"

Ruthanne was not able to answer. Her lips were trembling and she kept staring at the envelope. Seeing it, Chloe was pretty sure Ruthanne knew what they had found. Slowly, she nodded her head.

Greene opened the folder and pulled the contents out. He spread the letters out on the table. He even pulled the small photo album out of the folder and placed that in front of her as well.

"These are all addressed to a woman named Ruthie," Greene said. "I assume that is a nickname for Ruthanne. If I am wrong, please correct me."

Again, Ruthanne shook her head. "They're written to me."

"How long have you been keeping in touch with him?" Greene asked.

"Ten years or so," Ruthanne said. She took a moment and managed to stave off the emotional breakdown that she had seemed to be on the brink of having. She was finally able to look at Greene and Peterson. Now that she had been found out, she looked almost relieved. She sank into the chair and looked at them both with a sleepy sort of interest.

"How about the affair? When was that taking place?"

"For about eight months before…"

"Before what?" Peterson asked. "Before Gale Fine was murdered?"

"Yes," Ruthanne said, the word coming out of her mouth like venom.

"So we've learned that you were indeed involved with Aiden Fine," Peterson said. "Is there anything else you want to admit to?"

Ruthanne thought about this for about five seconds—long enough to make Chloe feel certain that she was trying to decide just *how much* the men in front of her knew. In the end, she decided to stay silent.

"We're going to note your silence," Peterson said, clearly irritated. "And I'm going to ask you a simple question: were you in any way involved with the death of Gale Fine seventeen years ago?"

"No."

"Are you sure? Maybe you started to have strong feelings for Aiden…maybe you wanted more than an affair and getting rid of Gale was the best way to get what you wanted."

In the observation room, Chloe was starting to cringe at the line of questioning. The impact of the questions was proof that she had no business being in that room. She was glad that Greene had put his foot down and insisted that she stay out of there.

"No, *no!"* Ruthanne said. But even through the glass, Chloe could see that something in Ruthanne was about to break.

Apparently, Greene took notice of this, too. He used a highly effective tactic and took the questioning elsewhere…for the moment.

"Okay, so we have one more item for you. Do you know a man named Alan Short?"

This question seemed to rock her. The emotion she was showing drained from her face for a moment. Again, she had showed her hand. She could deny it all she wanted but the reaction to the question gave them the real answer.

"No."

"You seemed shocked when the name came out of Agent Greene's mouth," Peterson told her. He then turned to Greene and added: "Want to show her the last item in your folder, Agent Greene?"

Greene reached into the folder and even before his hand came out, Ruthanne started talking again.

"Yes, I know him. We dated for a while and he—"

She stopped, uncertain of how to continue. Whatever it was inside of her that had been on the brink of collapsing or breaking was only seconds away from going nuclear.

"He what?" Greene asked. "Did he know Martin Shields? For that matter, did *you* know Martin Shields? Before the block party, I mean. I only ask because Alan Short's blood was found under Martin's fingernails. You do the math, Ms. Carwile. You do the math and—"

The sound that came out of Ruthanne's mouth was the wildest sound, the most guttural noise from a human throat, that Chloe had ever heard. And when she started talking again, it was a mix of shouting and weeping. She stood up from her chair so fast that Peterson's hand went to his service weapon at his hip.

"I had to get her out of the way! And we figured framing her for a murder would do it!"

"Had to get who out of the way?" Peterson asked.

Even before she answered, Chloe knew where this was going. She started to unwrap the entire thing in her head as each detail was revealed, and it took every ounce of strength within her not to rush into the interrogation room and break Ruthanne Carwile's fucking neck.

"Danielle! When he came back, she couldn't be here. So I had to have her removed..."

"When he came back?" Peterson asked. "I'm not following."

"When Aiden got out. He's up for parole in two years. I needed everything set up and ready when he got out. He wanted it that way, too. We planned this, you know? Get all of the distractions out of the way. No remnants of his old life...including Danielle. Because when she started digging into her mom's past...and calling the library...I got paranoid. I started sending the letters, trying to scare her off."

"Did you hire Alan Short to kill Martin Shields?" Greene asked.

"No. He just volunteered. I had to talk him into it near the end, but he was happy to do it."

"Jesus," Peterson murmured. "So you're telling me the man you're dating right now killed Martin Shields?"

Ruthanne opened her mouth to respond, but more wailing came out. She sank into the chair again and nodded. "Yes. And Martin scratched him in the fight. Right across the cheek."

"Where is he now?" Peterson asked, already reaching for his phone.

But then something dawned on Peterson—the very same thing that had come across Chloe's mind about thirty seconds earlier. He approached the table again, no longer worried about the location of Alan Short for the moment.

"Seventeen years ago…you were having an affair with Aiden Fine. *You* did it, didn't you? You killed Gale Fine. Pushed her down the stairs. And now, seventeen years later, you couldn't bring yourself to kill again. So you tried threatening letters to drive Danielle away. And when that didn't work, you found some idiot to do it for you…"

Ruthanne looked pitiful as she fought with an admission. Seeing her in a saddened state, as if she were the victim, enraged Chloe. She couldn't stand still any longer. In tears, she exited the observation room. She stormed the few steps to the interrogation room and threw the door open. She made a direct course for Ruthanne but was stopped instantly by Greene.

"Think about what you're doing," Greene said.

Chloe heard him, but just barely.

"Say it," Chloe said, her voice surprisingly calm. "Tell us what you did. Admit to it, you twisted bitch!"

Ruthanne looked Chloe in the eyes. Seeing genuine sorrow and regret there turned Chloe's stomach. "You had gone to the movies with a friend and Danielle was at the park with some kids, playing soccer. Your mom was at work. He called me over. Your mom came back home early with a headache, one of those migraines she used to get all the time. She walked in on us and there was an argument. I pushed her down the stairs…and to this day I don't know if I meant to—"

Chloe surged against Greene but he held her in place. *Get control,* Chloe thought. *Get control of yourself or you won't be able to see how this ends…*

"We decided to say he had done it, that it had been an accident. Involuntary manslaughter, saving me from jail, or so we thought. But it turned out to be second degree—a longer sentence. Still, he promised that when it was all over that he'd come for me, that we could be together. He wrote me letters after he was in jail…you only have some of them here," she said, slapping at the table.

Chloe gave one final surge, having to bite her lips to keep from screaming at her. Greene gently pushed her back and looked at Peterson.

"That's an admission of guilt," he said. "Can you handle it from here?"

"Yeah," Peterson said, still looking a little shocked.

Greene led Chloe back out into the hallway and quickly into the observation room before anyone could see the state she was in. She wiped tears away from her eyes and did her best to quickly regain control. Through the glass, she could hear Peterson reading Ruthanne her rights.

"Sorry," Chloe said. "God, I'm so sorry. I just couldn't stand here and…"

"It's okay," Greene said. "It might be on me a bit for even letting you this close to it. But I need you to tell me right now—are you okay? Can you finish this out with me?"

"Finish it?"

"Yes," Greene said. "If you're up to it, I think you should ride along and be there when we get Alan Short for the murder of Martin Shields."

The mere thought of this seemed to re-center her. It reminded her that she had not been asked to be a part of this investigation because of her history or her personal ties with it. Even after the shattering revelations she had just heard spilling for the mouth of Ruthanne Carwile, there was still a case to wrap up.

"Yes," she said, meaning it. "I'm good. When do we go?"

"As soon as she gives us a location," Greene said, hitching a thumb back toward the glass.

They both looked through it as Peterson finished reading the Miranda rights to the woman who, seventeen years later, had finally admitted to the murder of Chloe's mother.

CHAPTER THIRTY SIX

In the passenger seat of Greene's car, Chloe took a moment to text Danielle. She would have rather called, as texting seemed too impersonal, but she wasn't sure she could keep it together emotionally. And considering they were currently on the way to apprehend the man who had killed Martin, she thought it best that Agent Greene not see her lose her cool for the second time in less than an hour.

Ruthanne had given up Alan's location pretty much right away once she had been charged with the murder of Gale Fine. She'd given up much more than that, actually, letting them in on every little detail of their plan.

Since the night of the murder, Alan had been staying at a Super 8 motel in the small town of Maysville, a splat on the map between Pinecrest and Baltimore. He'd signed in under a fake name and had been paying cash. The plan, according to Ruthanne, was for them to split town and head to Alan's hometown of Charlottesville, Virginia, as soon as Danielle had been properly charged with Martin's murder.

Chloe did not relay all of that to Danielle, though. She kept it brief and to the point: **I know it's getting late. Found lots of answers and about to wrap up the last one, I think. I'll tell you everything when I get home. Just know this: it's looking very good for you.**

She received a response fairly quickly, just as the faint light of the Super 8 sign crept into view up ahead. There were two patrol cars ahead of them, compliments of the Pinecrest PD, with Detective Peterson in one of them. No one was running their flashers and they were keeping their speed to just slightly above the posted speed limit. They did not want to tip Alan Short off at all.

In fact, when they reached the parking lot, Agent Greene pulled in along the side, parking beside the front office. The two patrol cars went to the opposite end, one parking behind a large economy van and basically out of sight.

"I can't have you coming in," Greene said. "Johnson would have my head. But I want you to be part of it." He pulled out his phone and dialed up her number. "Answer this call and listen along.

I'll have it in the interior pocket of my jacket. Sorry…not very high tech, so it's the best we have."

With that, he pressed CALL and Chloe answered it right away. Greene then stepped out of the car and ran into the front office. She listened closely as Greene spoke with a woman at the front desk, letting her know what was about to go down. Without any fuss or trouble at all, she provided a key to the room Short was staying in.

As all of this went down, Chloe watched the other end of the lot. Peterson was out of the car, walking slowly to the open walkway that connected all of the rooms. When he was under the shadow of the awning covering the walkway, the three other officers followed behind. When they fell in line, one behind the other, they all placed their hands on the stock of their holstered sidearms.

Greene came out of the office, walking as if he belonged there. Anyone seeing him from the street might assume that he had simply rented a room for the night. He headed in the direction of Peterson and the waiting cops. As he moved toward them, they started moving forward. They met slightly off-center of the walkway with the door and window of Room 206 between them.

Through the phone, Chloe could hear Greene counting: *"One…two…three."*

Their entrance was not as dramatic as the busting down of the door. Instead, Green quickly stalked forward and inserted the key into the lock. As he did, Peterson and the officers fell in behind him, breaking into a flanked position with two on either side of him. Greene turned the lock and entered the room.

After that, Chloe could only listen, as the men entered the room and her phone was suddenly flooded with noise.

"On the ground, Mr. Short!" someone yelled.

"What the hell is this…?" came another voice, apparently that of Short.

"You're under arrest for the murder of—"

"Hands where I can fucking see them!"

"On the ground, *now*!"

There was a silence that felt uncomfortable even through the phone. It was broken by a single word shouted by Peterson.

"Gun!"

And then Chloe heard three gunshots through the phone. Someone screamed and then there was a sound like thunder.

Someone fell, Chloe thought. *Or a door was slammed.*

"I'm hit," someone said. "Just a graze though."

177

"Shit. Did we get him?"

"Don't know," said another voice, this one unmistakably Greene's.

Chloe sat up, sensing the situation getting out of control. *Someone was shot,* she thought. *But Short was apparently still lively enough to escape into the bathroom. What other door would there be to shut?*

Chloe felt a stir of instinct. She set her phone to the side and quietly got out of the car. She looked to the right, to the office and then the edge of the motel. It was barely illuminated in the glow of the Super 8 sign.

She walked quickly to the edge of the office and peered into the darkness behind the motel. She could see nothing, but she *did* hear a slight commotion. She went further into the dark alley beside the motel and started to make out movement farther down. And as she saw the movement, she heard a muted voice.

"Get out of there *now,* Mr. Short, or we *will* break the door down. You've shot a cop. Anything you do from this point out makes it that much worse for you."

Understanding what she was seeing further along in the darkened space behind the motel, Chloe hurried toward the movement. As she drew closer, she saw that her hunch was right. Alan Short was escaping through the small bathroom window. He was barely able to fit through, but he was already halfway out, his head dangling down as his left arm reached for the ground.

Chloe was unarmed, so when she saw the gun in Short's right hand, she hesitated. But only for a moment. She moved quickly, sticking to the side of the building. By the time she was close enough for Short to hear her footfalls, she was less than ten feet away from him.

He tried raising the gun but then started slipping through the window. Behind him, they both heard the sound of the bathroom door crashing down.

Chloe delivered a hard right-handed haymaker that took Alan Short hard in the side of his head. He slipped the rest of the way out of the window and fell to the pavement. Chloe acted right away, stomping down on his right wrist. As Short released the gun, she dropped down on his back. She planted a knee in the center of his back and drew his arms back hard.

He cried out in pain as she pulled backward. He wrestled against her but she had him pinned in a way where every movement applied more pressure to her hold.

She heard commotion from the edge of the motel, from where she had slunk toward the window. She was relieved to see Greene and Peterson running toward her. When they came to her side, she saw a grin of satisfaction on Greene's face.

"I'll yell at you about getting out of the car later," Greene said as he took over. "But for now, job well done."

Chloe stepped back as Greene applied handcuffs to Alan Short. And as Peterson read Short his rights, Chloe leaned against the wall. For a moment, she thought she might faint.

In the end, she had to fight back tears. It was a fight she was still having with herself even as she and Greene escorted Alan Short to Peterson's patrol car.

She did not realize just how large Alan Short was until she watched him bend down to fit into the back seat. Alan Short was a large man and the idea that she had pinned him to the ground sent a flood of accomplishment through her.

"It was her, wasn't it?" Short asked before Peterson closed the door. "She turned me over."

"If you're referring to Ruthanne Carwile, yes, she did. But only after we busted her for a murder seventeen years ago. Did you know about that?"

"Yeah, she told me. She has nightmares about it."

Good, Chloe thought.

"So she's been arrested, too?" Short asked.

"In the process," Peterson said. "Maybe we can find you two a cell together."

"To hell with that," Short said. "She's a wildcat in the sack, which is why I stuck with her for so long, but that bitch is straight up crazy."

"But yet you killed for her," Greene said. "Makes me wonder who's the *truly* crazy one."

With that, Peterson closed the door to end the conversation.

And as the door shut in Alan Short's face, Chloe couldn't help but feel as if it might even be the sound of a door closing within her own life—a door that she had often opened up in order to obsess over the past.

But she knew that before she could truly hope to have that door closed, she had to fill Danielle in on everything first.

It would be difficult and they'd probably both cry a lot.

She just hoped Danielle hadn't gone through all of the wine in the house while she had been alone. God knew they'd need some to get through the entire story.

CHAPTER THIRTY SEVEN

Two days later, as they sat in Chloe's car following Martin's funeral, Chloe handed her phone to Danielle. There was a news article up, from a link Agent Greene had sent her.

"Looks like it's official now," Chloe said.

Danielle took the phone and read over the article Chloe had just read. Chloe read it for a second time as well, just to experience it again. The headline read **Ex-girlfriend Cleared in Murder Case as Larger Conspiracy is Revealed**.

The article told most of the story that had been uncovered by Chloe and confessed by Ruthanne Carwile. Seventeen years ago, Ruthanne Carwile had killed Gale Fine when she came home to find Ruthanne and Aiden Fine in bed together. The murder was easily passed off as involuntary manslaughter—a simple push of aggression that caused Gale Fine to fall down the stairs. But in her guilt Ruthanne had confessed that she had done it on purpose. In court, though, a sentencing of second degree murder had been passed down.

Per her confession, Aiden had been horrified, and yet he had silently taken the blame for Ruthanne. She visited him once in prison, and he told her he did so because he felt guilty about their affair, and guilty that the affair had led to his wife's death, even if he had no hand in it. She had tried to make plans with Aiden, that when he got out of prison, they'd be together, but he refused until several years later, when he admitted he still loved Ruthanne and agreed she could start visiting him again.

Chloe wasn't able to read the entire thing again, though. Danielle seemed to tire of it before she came to the end. She closed the window out and handed the phone back to Chloe.

"If it ends with how Ruthanne kept tabs on Aiden Fine's rogue and troubled daughter—those words from Fox News this morning, by the way—I don't want to hear it. It creeps me out."

Chloe understood that. Truth be told, it creeped her out, too.

She caught Danielle looking back out at Martin's graveside. The service had been brief and the crowd turnout had been thin. Chloe still wasn't quite sure why Danielle had insisted on coming. Maybe because, despite all of the drama that had come with him in the end, the fake façade Martin Shields had showed her had been the closest Danielle had come to finding a man she trusted.

This might set that search back, Chloe thought.

"You know, I'm going to look for a new place to live starting tomorrow," Danielle said, still looking at the grave. "I can't go back to that apartment. I need to…*grow up,* I guess."

"You're welcome to come back to my house," Chloe said. "You can stay as long as you like. It's not like Steven is coming back anytime soon."

"You know that for sure?" Danielle asked.

"Yeah. He sent me a series of dates this morning, wanting to know when I'd be available to meet him. He wants the engagement ring back."

"Classy," Danielle said.

"But understandable."

Danielle sighed. "Do you feel any better now knowing that Dad was *basically* innocent in Mom's death?" she asked.

"No. If anything, I hate him more."

"You know what I hate?" Danielle said. "That the asshole has been cleared of his charges. He's going to be freed, isn't he?"

"I don't know," Chloe said. It was a true answer, though Peterson and Greene seemed to think it would only be a matter of time now that Ruthanne had confessed to everything.

"Let's get out of here," Danielle said.

Chloe started the car and pulled out of the lot. They'd been sitting there for fifteen minutes now, the service long since over.

Five minutes down the road, Danielle pressed the side of her head against the passenger window and started to cry. She cried openly and she cried hard.

Chloe had never seen this before, not in such a raw way. She had no idea what to do so she did what every sister-instinct in her demanded: she reached out and took her sister's hand.

Danielle took it and gave it a squeeze. Chloe drove on like that, with Danielle's hand in hers. She couldn't help but think of the two of them in the back of their grandmother's car seventeen years ago, holding hands while somewhere behind them their mother's body was taken to a morgue and their father was taken to prison.

For a moment, she felt trapped in a loop—the same loop that had brought her back to trying to understand why her mother had been killed. Now that they had answers, though, she hoped the loop would break and allow them both to, finally, escape.

EPILOGUE

5 months later…

She should have been excited about graduating. She should have been thrilled that she would no longer be an intern and would actually be carrying a badge and an ID that didn't need to come with an instructor or a special set of restrictions.

But what Chloe was most excited about was that she could see Danielle from her seat. She was tucked away in the nearly three thousand spectators in attendance but, as was usually the case with Danielle, somehow managed to stand out. She had started to grow her hair out. And even though it was still raven black, hiding their genetically similar blonde hair, Danielle looked just like their mother. Danielle caught her looking and gave a little wave. Chloe waved back and tried to remember a time in the past when she had ever felt such an outpouring of love and support from her sister.

From up on the stage, the commencement speaker stepped down. A smattering of applause filled the open yard, but not too much. The entire graduation ceremony had been much stuffier than Chloe had been expecting. Still, when the emcee stepped up and said, "And now for those graduating from the School of Evidence Response…" she felt like an excited high schooler, anxious to step out and experience the world.

The list of graduates for the Evidence Response Team was rather short. Chloe's name was the sixteenth called. As she got to her feet and headed for the stage, she thought back not to the sound of Peterson's door closing on Alan Short and not even of the numerous compliments Greene had given her after the case had been wrapped.

Instead, she thought of Danielle, crying against the passenger side window. That crying had come *after* the case had been wrapped—after they had gotten all of the answers to all of their questions about their mother's death. It was an example of how when things came to an end, it was not necessarily a *finality* to things.

Sometimes, things just kept going on and on. It was something she and Danielle had both come to terms with over the last five months.

Yet as she stepped down from the stage, diploma in hand, she also knew that sometimes the best way to bring an end to things was to focus on a new beginning. She did not believe in fresh slates to start over from, but she *did* believe that with enough drive, people could escape the chains of the demons of their past.

As she walked back to her seat, she spotted Agent Greene. He was sitting close to the stage with other agents who had served as instructors. The look of pride she saw on his face when their eyes met was beyond compare. She thought it might be what it felt like to have a parent so obviously proud of you.

She'd never know, of course. And that was fine with her, for the most part.

After all, she had a new beginning. She had lost her parents and her fiancé, and she had nearly lost her sister.

But that new beginning sat just ahead, easily within her grasp. Maybe whatever came next would shape her into something new, something better. Maybe it could shape her in a way that she had never dared to dream of while mired to her heartbreaking past.

She looked back at Danielle, still smiling and waving, and that future seemed as bright and as real as ever.

A NEIGHBOR'S LIE
(A Chloe Fine Psychological Suspense Mystery—Book 2)

"A masterpiece of thriller and mystery. Blake Pierce did a magnificent job developing characters with a psychological side so well described that we feel inside their minds, follow their fears and cheer for their success. Full of twists, this book will keep you awake until the turn of the last page."
--Books and Movie Reviews, Roberto Mattos (re Once Gone)

A NEIGHBOR'S LIE (A Chloe Fine Mystery) is book #2 in a new psychological suspense series by bestselling author Blake Pierce, whose #1 bestseller Once Gone (Book #1) (a free download) has over 1,000 five-star reviews.

FBI Evidence Response Team agent Chloe Fine, 27, still reeling from the secrets of her past, finds herself thrown into her first case: the murder of a nanny in a seemingly perfect suburban town.

Immersed in a world of secrets, of unfaithful couples, of pretense and artifice, Chloe soon realizes that anyone—and everyone—may be guilty. Yet at the same time, with her own father still in jail, she must battle her own demons and unravel her own secrets, which threaten to bring her down before her own career even begins.

An emotionally wrought psychological suspense with layered characters, small-town ambiance and heart-pounding suspense, A NEIGHBOR'S LIE is book #2 in a riveting new series that will leave you turning pages late into the night.

Book #3 in the CHLOE FINE series will be available soon.

Blake Pierce

Blake Pierce is author of the bestselling RILEY PAGE mystery series, which includes thirteen books (and counting). Blake Pierce is also the author of the MACKENZIE WHITE mystery series, comprising nine books (and counting); of the AVERY BLACK mystery series, comprising six books; of the KERI LOCKE mystery series, comprising five books; of the MAKING OF RILEY PAIGE mystery series, comprising two books (and counting); of the KATE WISE mystery series, comprising two books (and counting); and of the CHLOE FINE psychological suspense mystery, comprising two books (and counting).

An avid reader and lifelong fan of the mystery and thriller genres, Blake loves to hear from you, so please feel free to visit www.blakepierceauthor.com to learn more and stay in touch.

BOOKS BY BLAKE PIERCE

CHLOE FINE PSYCHOLOGICAL SUSPENSE MYSTERY
NEXT DOOR (Book #1)
A NEIGHBOR'S LIE (Book #2)

KATE WISE MYSTERY SERIES
IF SHE KNEW (Book #1)
IF SHE SAW (Book #2)

THE MAKING OF RILEY PAIGE SERIES
WATCHING (Book #1)
WAITING (Book #2)

RILEY PAIGE MYSTERY SERIES
ONCE GONE (Book #1)
ONCE TAKEN (Book #2)
ONCE CRAVED (Book #3)
ONCE LURED (Book #4)
ONCE HUNTED (Book #5)
ONCE PINED (Book #6)
ONCE FORSAKEN (Book #7)
ONCE COLD (Book #8)
ONCE STALKED (Book #9)
ONCE LOST (Book #10)
ONCE BURIED (Book #11)
ONCE BOUND (Book #12)
ONCE TRAPPED (Book #13)
ONCE DORMANT (book #14)

MACKENZIE WHITE MYSTERY SERIES
BEFORE HE KILLS (Book #1)
BEFORE HE SEES (Book #2)
BEFORE HE COVETS (Book #3)
BEFORE HE TAKES (Book #4)
BEFORE HE NEEDS (Book #5)
BEFORE HE FEELS (Book #6)
BEFORE HE SINS (Book #7)
BEFORE HE HUNTS (Book #8)
BEFORE HE PREYS (Book #9)

BEFORE HE LONGS (Book #10)

AVERY BLACK MYSTERY SERIES
CAUSE TO KILL (Book #1)
CAUSE TO RUN (Book #2)
CAUSE TO HIDE (Book #3)
CAUSE TO FEAR (Book #4)
CAUSE TO SAVE (Book #5)
CAUSE TO DREAD (Book #6)

KERI LOCKE MYSTERY SERIES
A TRACE OF DEATH (Book #1)
A TRACE OF MUDER (Book #2)
A TRACE OF VICE (Book #3)
A TRACE OF CRIME (Book #4)
A TRACE OF HOPE (Book #5)

92192169R00109

Made in the USA
Middletown, DE
06 October 2018